Little Lugosi

(a love story)

Douglas Ford

Madness Heart Press
2006 Idlewilde Run Dr.
Austin, Texas 78744

Cover by Luke Spooner

First Edition
www.madnessheart.press

Acknowledgments:

As always, my loving wife, Jerlin, helped make this book possible. She supports both my craft and my madness, and for that, I'm eternally grateful to her.

Thank you also to my publisher, John Baltisberger, for his support and faith in my writing. I'm also indebted to Desiree Byars, who did a tremendous job with the editing of this small book. She truly helped make it better.

Finally, thank you to my colleagues on the Venice campus of the State College of Florida. While Trevor, Mac, and the former Professor Barnswallow are inventions of my own imagination, the landscape and topography of Vissaria State College has a great deal in common with our campus and its close connection to wildlife. Sadly, land development has placed much of the surrounding habitat in jeopardy, and we see less and less of the wild pigs on our campus. I miss them, and the legacy of their presence inspired much of this book. This one is for them.

"Mark but this flea, and mark in this,
How little that which thou deniest me is;
It sucked me first, and now sucks thee,
And in this flea our two bloods mingled be;
Thou know'st that this cannot be said
A sin, nor shame, nor loss of maidenhead,
Yet this enjoys before it woo,
And pampered swells with one blood made of two,
And this, alas, is more than we would do."

--John Donne

ONE

Madeline called it Little Lugosi. She bought it from a medical supply company after talking to Trevor about how they didn't have any pets and how she considered that a damn shame.

A couple needed a pet, she explained. For almost a week, she kept hammering this point.

Trevor thought a dog, perhaps. Maybe. But he spent a day at work thinking about how he never really wanted a dog, not really. He didn't care for their fur, their smells, or their shedding bodies.

But he loved Madeline and her crazy, unpredictable ways. As he spent his workday landscaping the greenery surrounding the college, he thought about how he feared losing Madeline.

Sometimes he wondered what she saw in him, and during his darker moods, he speculated that she secretly found him predictable, his taste in music old-fashioned, his sense of style basic to the point of dullness. He should just give in to the idea of a pet.

But before any further discussion could take place, a box arrived in the late afternoon mail, and its delivery required a signature. The mailman held the box while Trevor signed. Trevor eyed the box, noticing the words, *For Medical Use Only.* He stopped in the middle of signing his name.

"I didn't order anything medical," he said.

The postal worker turned the package so Trevor could see the name printed on the label: Madeline's name. This meant he had no choice but to accept the package.

"Be careful with it," said the postal worker. "It contains living matter."

"Living matter?" Trevor asked, but the postman, no longer having any interest once he delivered the package, had already started down the walkway from the apartment.

Gently, Trevor shook the package. From inside came the sound of something swishing around. He set it on the card table they used for meals and didn't go near it. Something about it unnerved him.

When Madeline came home later that evening from her shift at the retirement home, she saw the box and made an excited noise. From the kitchen, Trevor watched her open it with a knife while he stirred a port of boiling water for mac and cheese.

Eventually, Madeline held up what looked like the kind of clear plastic container restaurants used for carry-out soup orders. It contained clear liquid and something black clinging to its side.

"Meet our new pet," she said, inviting him to come closer.

"What is it?"

"A leech. Anyone can order one."

"I don't get it," said Trevor. He really didn't. He continued to stir the boiling water.

"This is the perfect pet for us," she said. "No messes. No shedding. Just occasional feedings. Ideal for a working couple like us. Come see."

Trevor left the bubbling water and approached close enough to regard the black thing inside the container. It didn't seem to move at first, but then he realized it was flexing itself, almost pulsing on the side of the plastic. Madeline held out the container as if she expected him to take it.

"What do you mean by 'feedings'?" he asked.

"You know what a leech eats, don't you?"

Trevor did. He just didn't want to answer out loud and so let his silence say it for him.

She said, "I have a name picked out already. Little Lugosi. I want to take him out of the container. You think it's too soon?"

Trevor assumed she meant too soon to take him out of the container. Should it *ever* come out of its watery home? Not that he had an opinion about that. He finished cooking the mac and cheese and served the two of them a bowl each. The plastic container with Little Lugosi sat on the table between them.

"I think he's hungry," Madeline said between bites of food.

"I don't know how you can tell." Trevor

wished they could eat without the leech between them. "They just sold you that even though you're not a doctor?"

"Obviously. And I do work in the medical industry."

"You empty bedpans for old people," Trevor said.

"That's the medical industry." She put down her fork and pushed her bowl away. "I don't feel right about eating in front of him. I'd really like to take him out. Do you think I should?"

"No," said Trevor, chewing.

"You're not very adventurous."

"I can be. Sometimes."

"We'll see," she said. She left the table and returned with a Sharpie. She picked up the container and began writing something on its clear exterior. Once completed, she turned the container so he could see what'd shc'd written in neat cursive. *Little Lugosi.* She seemed to wait for a specific reaction, and when she didn't get what she expected, she explained the name came from some old movie actor who played Dracula. But Trevor never heard of him. He regarded how the name looked and struggled to fake enthusiasm about it.

"I'm going to take him out," she said. "I want to hold him. I want to put him on you."

Trevor considered his words. He knew this was what she meant when she said they would see how adventurous he could be. He hated how he would sound when he answered. He kept his voice low. "I don't think so."

"Let's go over some things," she said. "You have high cholesterol. You have high blood pressure. You eat," she gestured at the bowls in front of them, "like shit. There's a reason why medical companies sell Little Lugosis. This would be *good* for you. You never go to the doctor. You hurt all the time and barely want to do anything but stay at home and watch TV. I'm doing this for us, not just so we have something take care of, but for its medical benefits."

But Trevor kept saying no. He cleared the dishes, feeling Madeline's stare as he did so. He felt so old suddenly. When had that happened? Only four years younger than him, Madeline looked half his age, and she acted like it too.

They went to bed early that night, barely talking to one another.

The next morning, when he awoke, Trevor found her already gone.

Eventually, as he got himself ready for work, he noticed something else.

The container with Little Lugosi had disappeared.

TWO

Trevor hoped Madeline woke up with second thoughts about keeping the leech. Maybe she flushed him down the toilet and threw the container into the dumpster outside their apartment.

At work, he thought more about offering to get a dog. Or maybe a cat made more sense, given the size of their apartment. He spent most of the day re-sodding a portion of the grass that grew around the perimeter of the college campus. It happened quite frequently he'd roll into work and find the landscaping in utter disarray, and the damage always seemed to occur suddenly overnight.

According to Mac, Trevor's workmate, they could thank a gang of marauding wild pigs that lived in the woods surrounding the college. "They come out at night and feast on all our work, all this back-breaking work," Mac said, practically throwing dirt with his shovel as they tried to level out the ground.

Trevor took his word for it. Other than a stray deer and an inordinate number of rabbits, he seldom saw any wildlife of note wander out from the trees. In fact, he preferred to not know what lived in the acres of woodland that surrounded the campus. Things he couldn't see unnerved him, and he didn't like the thought of creatures hidden behind trees, watching him.

"We've got to do something about it. Take some hard measures," said Mac.

Trevor would nod and keep raking up the mess so they could lay down new sod. Talking just tired him out. Maybe, he thought, if not a dog or cat, then a pig—a pet pig. People had those, didn't they? Mac would love that if he spoke that out loud. The other groundskeeper pretty much hated all the woodland creatures, though for reasons Trevor couldn't fathom, he treated the rabbits with a quiet tolerance.

When Trevor took a breather, he'd watch the female students walking between the campus's three main buildings, their tan legs leading up to shorts that seemed to get shorter and more revealing every year. He made sure not to stare too long as he didn't want to become known as the creepy groundskeeper, and besides, his heart really did belong to Madeline. After the iciness of the night before, he dreaded all the more the possibility of losing her.

But when she beat him home that day, he found her all smiles, the tension from the night before seemingly forgotten.

He also saw she held the container with Little Lugosi.

"I have the best story," she said, beaming at him.

She told him how she brought Little Lugosi with her to work and how she kept him hidden with her lunch all that day, thinking maybe she would take him out at some point for a feeding.

Trevor raised his eyebrows. "No, let me tell

you," she said, going on to describe a patient named Mr. Driscoll. Trevor had heard about Mr. Driscoll before, a sad old man already into his hundreds who never had any visitors and seemed to have no surviving family. A while ago, Madeline had taken a shine to Mr. Driscoll, and now she reminded Trevor how the old man had stopped talking and would barely move a muscle all day. He remained completely unresponsive, practically comatose, barely even registering when Madeline moved him around in the bed to assist him in one of his watery bowel movements.

"I've always felt sorry for him," Trevor said, mainly to make Madeline happy. He rarely, if ever, thought of Mr. Driscoll. During his rare visits to Madeline at work, he tried not to stay long and resisted meeting any of the residents when Madeline offered. The idea of growing old and dying scared him.

"I know you do," she said, "so do I. It breaks my heart seeing someone like that. But today I got this idea. I thought he probably wouldn't even notice if I took Little Lugosi out and let him have a small taste. So, when I was alone, I did it. Don't look at me like that, don't judge me. Remember, there are medical benefits to this sort of thing."

This news held Trevor speechless for a moment. "You violated him, Madeline."

"No, no, see, I didn't. I left Little Lugosi on him for just a minute. Just enough time for him to latch on. Okay, maybe it was more like five minutes. But you know what? When I pulled off Little Lugosi, Mr. Driscoll smiled. Not only that, but he actually spoke. The first words out of that man in I don't know how long. He looked at me and called me Rose."

"That's not your name."

"No, it's his daughter's, I think. My guess is she's dead along with rest of his family. That's what his records say, at least—no surviving relatives. But the point is that he actually spoke. I went and got the staff doctor, and he couldn't believe it. He said he'd practically given up on Mr. Driscoll. Get this: Mr. Driscoll ate some solid food after that. He even sat up and watched *Wheel of Fortune* while I fed him."

Trevor said, "What happens when he tells the doctor that you put a leech on him? You'll get fired."

"He had no idea I did that, and he'll never find out. It only left a little mark. And besides, look at Little Lugosi."

Trevor regarded the tiny black thing in the container. It wiggled, appearing more animated. Something else had changed. It looked larger, fatter, happier, if one could even call a leech happy. *No*, Trevor corrected himself, it simply looked pleased with itself.

That comes from love, thought Trevor. *It knows it's loved. It can feel it.*

He looked at Madeline, and she looked back, a beaming smile on her face.

THREE

Every subsequent day, Madeline took Little Lugosi to work. Each day she returned home with him, still floating in his clear container, happy and sated. The leech grew longer and fatter.

She wouldn't say whether or not she continued to let it feed on Mr. Driscoll. Trevor didn't ask either. He didn't want to know. Sometimes he imagined he ought to call the retirement home to tell them what he suspected Madeline of doing. During those moments, he thought about how difficult their lives would become if she lost her job—or worse, if she got arrested. He never made that call.

One afternoon, she came home in tears.

"Mr. Driscoll died," she said.

The look on her face caused Trevor to draw back, his breath to come up short. The people she cared for often died of course, their bodies stricken by the ravages of age and disease, but never had he seen her react with such sadness. Trevor tried to say something comforting, but he only managed to generate the usual platitudes people hear—*I'm sure he's in a better place; he lived a long and rewarding life; his suffering is over*, and so on. When he tried to touch her, she swiped his hand away.

A terrible thought occurred to him. "You don't think you killed him, do you? With *that*?" He meant Little Lugosi.

"It was making him better," she said, though Trevor thought he could hear doubt in her voice. "I know it was."

Gently, Trevor tried telling her what he learned the day before when he took his lunch break in the college's library. Using a computer outside of anyone's line of sight (the college had rules forbidding a groundskeeper from using resources intended for students), he looked up information

19

about leeches and learned they basically had one medical benefit—to help with blood clotting. "I don't know how it works exactly. I just understood enough to know they don't reverse aging or cure dementia. It just doesn't work that way."

"You don't think I know that?" she said. The way she narrowed her eyes made him wither. His mouth went dry. "You don't think I don't know something as basic as that? But it was also to help him feel something. To remind him he was alive! For him to feel connected to something! It's about the *humors*, Trevor. The goddamn *humors*, the fluids in his body, the bile and blood, the piss and shit. I kept him fed, I cleaned him up. *I knew him.* As for you? You don't know shit."

Later, she slept on the couch and refused his entreaties to come to bed, no matter how contrite he acted.

The humors. He had no idea what she meant by that. Maybe, he thought as he tried to sleep, he'd look it up at some point. In truth, he felt some relief at hearing about the old man's death. No telling what consequences Madeline would've faced if someone found out her secret. Nothing good, most likely unemployment, maybe even prison. He decided the time had come for Little Lugosi to go away. Tomorrow they'd flush him. He'd convince her of the wisdom of his decision. *Their* decision, he corrected himself, because he'd make her see reason. Maybe he'd even say the kind of things that would result in her deciding this for herself, and then he could just agree.

In the morning, he felt relief when she spoke to him, and he believed the thaw he hoped for had indeed arrived.

"I want to talk about Little Lugosi," she said over a bowl of cereal.

Trevor nodded and waited for more.

She said, "Mr. Driscoll is alive inside Little Lugosi. He's a part of him now. That little creature represents something bigger than you and me together. Something … I don't know, eternal?"

Trevor searched her face, looking for clues as to what he should say. Her face remained fixed, her brow furrowed in thought while her eyes shifted side to side just slightly, seeming to dance in barely perceptible movement. He tried to imagine the brain activity behind those eyes. *Eternal*—what the fuck? A long time ago, they both agreed not to give credence to such notions. When Madeline's father died, Trevor helped her collect the ashes, despite the fact that he never liked the old man and his cracks about Trevor's complexion, referring to him as "that colored boy my baby girl picked up at the fair." Nevertheless, he stood next to her on a jetty stretching out into the Gulf of Mexico, helping her release the ashes into the wind. Some of the ashes blew back into their faces, and they both wound up coughing like three-pack-a-day smokers. But they laughed it off, joking that they might have ingested some of Madeline's father's racism in the process. A second later, Madeline got serious and pronounced the end of the private ceremony with a terse, "Well, I guess that's it," and they both left the scene to share some fries and a soda. Perhaps this business about *eternity* signified something unresolved.

"No. We have to get rid of it," Trevor said. Even to himself, he sounded weak.

She met him with an expression of horror. No words yet.

"We could get a dog," he continued. "Or a cat. Shit, a rabbit. Anything. Something we can pet. Hell, maybe we should have a kid."

"A *kid*. You want to have a *kid*? You think a *kid* will save us?"

His turn to look horrified. Had they approached some marital precipice without him even realizing it? Did they *need* saving?

"You want to put a kid inside me, and you don't have the decency to consider what I want? No matter how small?" she asked.

"Hold on," he said, but she moved quickly, stepping away from the table. He panicked, thinking she meant to head for the door and out of his life. Instead, she approached a shelf where she'd set Little Lugosi's plastic container.

"This," she said, "is what I need right now. This means more to me than any dog or cat or bunny or *kid* could mean to me right now. And if we don't feed him, he will die. Look me in the eye and tell me his life doesn't mean anything."

"All right," Trevor said, "his life doesn't mean anything."

Frowning, she studied his face. He felt that precipice under his feet, and the earth began to sway. He watched as she opened the container's lid and dipped her finger inside the liquid. Later, Trevor would wonder if he imagined it, but it seemed the black nub of the creature's body actually swam toward her finger, as if she'd somehow trained the thing.

Holding the creature delicately, she used her teeth to roll up the sleeves of her shirt, revealing several tiny black bruises on the inside of her arm. On an area still marked by her usual paleness she placed Little Lugosi, and Trevor watched in fascination as it spread itself over her skin and began to suck. A smile formed on Madeline's lips. Like a cat, she blinked slowly, in the throes of pleasure.

A few minutes ticked off that clock while Little Lugosi remained latched. Then she said, "Get me a pencil."

Trevor failed to respond immediately, his

attention fixed on the creature drawing sustenance, so Madeline commanded him a second time. He found a pencil on the coffee table and brought it to her.

"You have to perform this little procedure *very* carefully," she said as she used the nub of the pencil to release Little Lugosi from where he'd fixed himself to her. Blood quickly welled from the spot. Trevor watched as Madeline put her arm to her lips and cleaned off what Little Lugosi left behind.

"Your turn," she said to him. She held out the pencil to him, the black form writhing on its tip, clearly excited by the feeding, anxious for him now. When he hesitated, she said something mysterious—a memorized chant or a song, maybe a spell of some sort. Not that he would know. It went: "It sucked me first, and now sucks thee / And in Little Lugosi, our two bloods mingled be."

She smiled a smile Trevor couldn't help returning.

To the words she just spoke, Trevor added his own: "And Mr. Driscoll's blood too, I suppose."

She shook her head as if he just spoke nonsense and added her own addendum: "Oh, stay, three lives in one leech spare, / Where we almost, nay more than married are / This leech is you and I, and this / our marriage bed, and marriage temple is."

"I don't get it," said Trevor.

"It's just something I found in a book, only changed up a bit. There's just you and me. Little Lugosi is the vessel." She smiled again, and Trevor felt a glimmer of hope that everything was all right. He hoped so, at least.

Reluctantly, he held out his arm, and Little Lugosi began to suck.

FOUR

The pain in his arm woke him up several times that night, but at least they went back to sleeping together. By the glow of his bedside clock, he studied the mark left by Little Lugosi, and he recalled how it latched on to him—not an unpleasant feeling at first. It even felt sort of pleasurable, like an intense kiss. He watched in fascination as it sucked and sucked, its form writhing and pulsing in its form of ecstasy. But in seconds, the pleasure turned into sharp pain, and he felt the urge to swipe it away or to tear it off. The pain only grew, and he began to feel light-headed before finally saying, "Okay, that's enough."

Madeline had taken her time removing Little

Lugosi, once more using the pencil to gently release the creature and cooing to it as she did so. Trevor needed a Band-Aid once it was finally over.

Later, they had sex. The ferocity of their coupling made Trevor hesitate to call it lovemaking, a term he abhorred anyway. Madeline gripped his waist with her legs and bucked against him, coming several times before he finally spent himself inside of her, and even then, she didn't seem satisfied.

"Let me see your arm," she said as he lay panting next to her, and he obeyed her request. She tore off the Band-Aid and put her mouth to the wound left by Little Lugosi. She began sucking, and the pain roared back, forcing him to pull away.

This action left a spot of blood on her lip. She smiled in a sleepy sort of way. "What would it feel like," she asked, "if we put Little Lugosi on the base of your cock? Right on that pulsing vein?"

Trevor grimaced and looked at her with incomprehension, but before he could craft a suitable reply, her eyelids grew heavy and she drifted off to sleep.

As Trevor lay awake, studying the wound

by the clock light, a sound drew his attention. A clatter from the bathroom.

"You hear that?" he asked, but Madeline snored softly.

More clatter followed, louder this time, followed by what sounded like footsteps.

The shape of a pale old man appeared in the corner of the room, stooped and skeletal. Though the darkness hung heavy, Trevor could see the form of something dangling from the man's legs, and he knew then that this old man who'd appeared wore no clothing. In the shadows, it looked like a heavy leech dangling from his groin.

Then a voice: "Rose?"

Until he heard the shape speak, Trevor mistrusted his vision. Frantic, he turned on the light.

In the resulting illumination, he saw nothing there.

He only succeeded in waking up Madeline. "The fuck?" she said.

Still frightened, Trevor found himself blabbering incoherently. She looked at him as if trying to understand why he'd do something so rude and sudden. Then she looked down at the sheets. "Oh, fuck," she said.

Blood puddled where she lay. It smeared her thighs. Trevor's mind immediately went to an attack of some kind, a violation. More incoherent speech, until she shut him up.

"I got my period," she said. "That's all it is. Goddammit. It wasn't due for weeks."

FIVE

Instead of sleeping in the next morning like he preferred to do on a Saturday, Trevor got out of bed early to go join Mac like he promised he would. Mac wanted them to meet back on the campus so they could do something about the pigs, once and for all. Without fail, those pigs came out every night, and the destruction they caused had continued to mount to such an intolerable degree that Mac insisted they needed to take extra measures, though Trevor didn't know what sort of measures he meant exactly.

Such prospects didn't excite him, but after suffering through the nightmare or vision or whatever it was from the night before, he decided that getting out of the apartment for the morning might do him some good. He left Madeline sleeping in the middle of the blood-stained sheets. It looked like quite a lot of blood, in fact, and if he hadn't stopped to verify that she continued to breathe regularly, he might have thought that she'd died from some horrible accident. The female body mystified him, how it could just bleed on its own accord once a month and still function. He never stopped to consider that until now. A weird thought occurred to him—that if his own body could just let go of everything and bleed like that once in a while without killing him, he might not feel so bottled up all the time.

He found Mac waiting for him at the college outside the facilities building, his back against the side of his hearse-black pickup. On his head, Mac sported a cowboy hat, a different look from the baseball cap he wore on a workday. To Trevor, Mac looked ready for line dancing or a rodeo. Mac approached him with two rifles, one for each of them.

"Afraid I only told you part of the story," said

Mac.

"Not the Minister bullshit again," said Trevor.

"He's real, I swear."

Mac referred to the existence of a giant boar, one that purportedly lived in the more remote region around the campus. Trevor didn't know why they called it *the Minister*, and Mac never had a clear answer, but he spoke of it with the awed reverence due to some kind of unfathomably large animal that had eluded hunters for years. Pick any disreputable bar in Vissaria County and you could find some drunk with a story about hunting the Minister, along with tales about how many men it had killed and how supernaturally long it had lived. Apparently, the stories about the Minister went far back in Vissaria County history, so far, in fact, they challenged credulity, but Mac swore to the truth of the stories, including the ones about how it had developed a taste for human flesh. Mac even claimed to have seen it on multiple occasions. "It watches you with what I can only describe as human intelligence," Mac liked to say.

Following Mac toward the thick row of pines

that stood sentry around the campus, Trevor held the rifle in the crook of his arm, hoping he looked more comfortable with it than he felt. People assumed he knew his way around firearms. What else would one expect from a groundskeeper in the southern clime? Not that he couldn't shoot— he knew how weapons worked—but he didn't buy the God and guns bullshit that Mac liked to preach. According to Mac, religion and guns went together like peanut butter and jelly.

As they maneuvered through the brush, and an especially stubborn pepper tree that seemed to have exploded amongst the pines, Mac said, "I saw him early this week. Right over there." Trevor squinted in the direction he pointed, fighting the droplets of the sweat that had already blurred his vision and barely making out a slight slope in the land where a fallen tree crossed what little path they had. "Another time, I saw him that way. Yonder, there's a clearing I think he likes. You'll believe in him when you see him. It ain't just his size, it's his color too. Blacker than night, even his tusks. He ain't natural. You can see it reflected in

34

his eyes."

"If you say so," Trevor said. He thought about Madeline at home, wondering if she was still lying there in her own blood. Maybe his recollection exaggerated how much blood came out of her, but now he wondered if he ought to have woken her to make sure she didn't need medical help. Of course, she might have called him stupid for worrying about a goddamn period. He ought to have stayed home. He didn't like it out here.

Not seeming at all bothered by the humidity or the bugs that swarmed around Trevor, Mac went on: "After I saw him the second time, I started having a dream. Three nights in a row, the same dream. God talking to me." Mac stopped walking and turned to face Trevor, as if to prove his seriousness. "God appeared to me, and He looks just like He does in the paintings—an old man with a long white beard. The last time I had the dream, He said to me, 'Mac, you get Trevor out here on the weekend. I hereby commission you to kill that evil pig and set fire to its corpse.'"

The sun continued to rise, but wisps of

morning still clung to the vast sea of green around them. Trevor took a deep breath as he pondered how to reply. "We still hunting the other pigs?"

"You see them and have a clear shot, you take it. But save plenty of ammo for the Minister. You'll need a lot to take him down. He's got to burn."

"I'm not eating anything we kill," said Trevor.

"That girl of yours turning you into a vegetarian?"

Trevor slowed down, nearly stopping as he wondered where that came from. Madeline ate meat. He'd never implied otherwise. Maybe Mac, a bachelor apparently, assumed all women were vegetarians who plotted to turn men into plant eaters. He thought it best to simplify his answer and simply said no, she hadn't succeeded in doing that.

"Well, either way, I wouldn't recommend you eat the Minister's carcass. It's diseased, no doubt. Full of Satan's worms. You want to check the clearing I mentioned, or that hollow down yonder?"

Trevor said he'd take the hollow.

"More likely you'd see the Minister in the clearing," Mac said.

Trevor repeated he'd take the hollow.

"Stay in shouting distance," Mac said. "I hear you yelling, I'll come running."

"Same."

As Mac went off in the other direction, Trevor started down a section of sloping terrain, slipping on uneven ground. Lower still, thin veils of fog became visible, vestiges of the morning the sun hadn't finished burning away. The fog seemed to rise the further he descended, and it surprised him how the terrain seemed to change, given the characteristic flatness of their region. The fog made things harder to see too, and for the first time, Trevor started to feel afraid. He resisted the urge to call out to Mac, to test how far his voice would carry or how long it would take the other man to cross the distance that separated them. He thought again of Madeline, the warmth of her body, but also that drying puddle of blood. How could she stand to sleep on it?

Deeper into the hollow, he heard an unfamiliar

sound. Grunting. Something panting.

Trevor stopped walking and imagined the god who visited Mac in his sleep. He tried to call upon this god now, but the image described by his fellow groundskeeper, the old man with the long flowing beard, merged with what he saw clatter out of his bathroom the night before: the wrinkled, naked phantom. Just a dream too, he reminded himself. He tried walking back the way he came, but the thickening fog distorted his sense of direction, and he found himself going in circles. The grunting and panting seemed to increase in volume no matter which way he turned. His disorientation increased until the ground began to slope and he stumbled into a clearing where the layers of fog began to lift.

At first, he just saw the water, a large pond he didn't know existed back there.

Then he saw the other thing near its bank, an image he struggled to resolve in his mind.

A giant form covered in coarse black hair giving birth to some pale, writhing creature.

This event took place on a carpet of grass surrounding the tea-colored water of the pond.

Trevor blinked, still trying to make sense of what he saw.

Then he recognized what he stumbled upon.

Not birth.

A giant black pig mounting a naked woman with long black hair.

Rutting.

Trevor tried calling for Mac, but he could only make a low, desperate sound, barely audible.

But loud enough for the pig and the woman to hear him. They both looked in his direction.

As if startled by his presence, the woman began to struggle under the pig, and Trevor raised his rifle, for an awful moment thinking the rutting would turn into something far worse, more violent. If Trevor needed to fire the gun, he couldn't guarantee that he wouldn't hit the woman by mistake. But before he could do anything, the woman managed to squirm her way out from under the pig and she bolted for the tree-line, carried by long, bare legs, where she disappeared quickly.

The pig didn't give chase. Instead, it regarded

Trevor with what he could only interpret as a very human loathing, anger at having its mating interrupted in so rude a fashion. Its tumescent tool looked shiny and irritated, and it dripped something foul onto the ground. Its curved tusks shone black in the morning sun.

Trevor could understand now what Mac meant by the human eyes of the Minister.

Then the monstrous pig bolted up the same path used by the woman, disappearing into the forest behind her.

Trevor tried calling for Mac, managing to produce only a flaccid sound, his mind wracked with questions about what he'd just witnessed.

Like how could this be real?

And that woman with the long black hair, the shape of her body one he recognized.

Had he just seen Madeline run naked into the woods after doing something unspeakable with a wild pig even though he'd left her at home not so long ago?

SIX

Later, once they found each other and mutually agreed to end the hunt without a single shot fired, Mac tried to talk Trevor into a beer, but Trevor refused, explaining he needed to get home immediately.

"You sure?" Mac said. "You don't look right. You saw him, didn't you—the Minister. I didn't hear any shots. He scare you?"

Trevor grunted a half-hearted affirmation. He blacked out after he saw what he saw, as if his brain just couldn't take it, and Mac had found him sitting alone deeper in the woods, his back leaning against the ruined foundation of some old, long-forgotten building. Trevor didn't remember walking there and couldn't recall how he came across it.

Mac had to snap his fingers several times in front of his face before Trevor showed any awareness of Mac's presence. Surmising that he must've lost his way through the fog, Trevor asked him the time.

Over two hours had gone by according to Mac, thanks in part to all the time he wasted looking for Trevor. Nodding toward the horizon, Mac said, "Thought I'd have to pull you out of the pond yonder. When I couldn't find you, I thought you fell in and drowned. Good thing I didn't jump in and check." He regarded Trevor with a grave expression. "Leeches," he added. "Pond is full of goddamn leeches. I seen a pig come out of that water once with leeches hanging off him like Christmas ornaments."

That prompted Trevor to get to his feet. "I need to go."

The trek back occurred in reverse order, Mac pulling up the rear this time, Trevor moving almost too fast for him to keep up.

"Beer another time?" Mac asked with Trevor nearly out of earshot.

"Yeah. Sure." He left Mac plenty confused, along with a scowl that expressed doubt he'd ever keep that promise.

Later, he found Madeline where he left her, still in bed, but awake now and sitting up with the television on.

"What?" she asked, apparently sensing the stare he directed at her from the doorway.

The sheets under her remained soiled with dried blood.

"I know," she said, misinterpreting his stony silence. "I ought to clean this up. I'm just feeling lazy."

She shifted and let the covers fall away, her body still naked. She gestured for him to join her, but Trevor remained in place, studying her legs, the curves of her body, looking for dirt and bruises, any signs of her coupling in the woods. A darkened stain of blood marked her thighs, but otherwise, she looked clean. Trevor thought about what he witnessed in the woods and his vision the night before of the old man, for the first time in his life beginning to doubt his own sanity. Sighing, he crawled into bed next to her, feeling her arms go around him.

"What is it?" she asked. She repositioned herself so his head could rest on her shoulder. "You take care of those pigs?"

Hesitating for a moment, Trevor said, "Yeah, we took care of them."

"Didn't kill them, I hope."

When he breathed, Trevor heard a faint wheeze come from his chest. Maybe he needed a doctor. "Just ran them off."

"They'll come back, you know. Wild pigs get a taste for something, they don't go away."

He lifted his head and studied her.

"I had a dream last night," she continued, "the best, most beautiful dream of my life. It was Mr. Driscoll, not really alive, but somehow resurrected. He came in through the window, floating on a carpet of light. He came to tell me that there is a heaven and I'd join him there some day. I mean, you along with me, of course. Even in my dream

I argued, saying there's no such thing as heaven, but he offered his hand to me, and I took it, letting him enfold me inside the light of his body. It felt like a kiss, the warmest kiss a human could receive, and he showed me the heaven we could all share some day. I wanted to stay there, but he told me I couldn't, not yet, and I cried. I cried so much. And he kissed me again. He said I needed to stay on earth so I could get pregnant and have a kid."

She twisted her head so she could see his reaction, read his thoughts. Trevor felt acid in the back of his throat. He got up to find the antacids they kept on the dresser. As he chewed, he regarded the blood on the sheets, how it had turned brown like the brittle roots of a dead tree.

"We need to clean this up," he said. "We're not rich. We can't just go out and buy new sheets."

"We can think about it, right? A kid? I mean, I know I've said other things about this before. I might be changing my mind."

Trevor grunted as he began pulling off the sheets. He felt tired, but Madeline made only half-hearted attempts to help him as he rolled the sheets

45

into a ball to make a trip to the laundry room. Grabbing a handful of quarters, he made the trip alone.

When he returned, he found Madeline dressed in the living room, rearranging a bookshelf they kept mounted on the wall for pictures and the few books they owned. It no longer held those objects. Instead, it became the seat for two burning candles, and between them sat the container holding Little Lugosi.

In silence, he watched her as she positioned everything carefully.

To Trevor, it looked like an altar.

SEVEN

For a time, they managed to avoid the subject of a kid at home; while at work, Trevor stayed too busy for much talk about the Minister. On the Sunday after their big hunt, Mac kept sending Trevor texts demanding to know if he felt okay and fishing for information about exactly what went down in that hollow when they separated. *I know u saw him*, one of Mac's messages read, *let's meet up next week with a plan of action!! Maybe get someone else to go with us!!*

Trevor didn't respond to any of these texts, and when the work week started, they had plenty to do because the pigs went at it with vengeance.

"The provost wants to hire out a crew to hunt

the pigs down," Mac told him. "I said we'd handle it."

Temperatures went into the nineties that week, and while they shoveled away ruined grass, Trevor hoped to keep the talking to a minimum. But he needed to respond. "We'd handle what? The pigs, or getting a crew together to do it for us?"

He wiped the sweat from his forehead and turned to hear the answer. Mac's eyes had turned toward the woods hiding the pond where Trevor experienced his incident. By this point, Trevor had rejected everything he witnessed that morning. As far as it concerned him, it simply hadn't happened. None of it. He explained it to himself this way: the leech caused hallucinations. In fact, that upraised mark on his arm refused to heal. It still bothered him. It must've sucked so much blood out of him that he went on their expedition too light-headed and simply saw things that weren't there.

Mac said, "I just told them we'd take care of it. You and me. We need to get back on the hunt."

"I don't know. I don't get paid enough to be spending my weekends searching for a mythical pig."

"It's not mythical. Look at this damage." Mac used his rake to gesture to ground under their feet. "Does this look mythical? It's real, this land, and it's cursed. I'm going to get us some help."

"Some help, you say," Trevor said, processing.

"A professor here. Anthropology. Or archeology. Whatever they call it. He's got the kind of background we need to end this."

"They teach you how to make pig traps in archeologist school?"

Mac leaned on his rake and regarded the scene around them as if intending to find a hidden spy in their midst. Then he spat something brown and acrid on the ground, a notable color since Mac, to Trevor's knowledge, didn't chew tobacco. The cracks in his leathery skin seemed to open up as he sighed, as if he required an alternative to normal breathing. Many times, Trevor had tried to estimate the age of his partner, but he found the task impossible.

"This ground has a history older than you and me combined," Mac said without giving any clue

49

to what sum that would come to. "The Minister too. He's older than us. We need someone who knows its history."

"We've got a hard enough job to do," said Trevor, almost adding that, at present, Mac, with all his talking, had left him to do that job alone.

"And we're doing it. Every day. The same thing. Don't you get tired of it?"

Now came Trevor's turn to stop and lean against his rake. Mac regarded him with the gaze of bright blue eyes. They let the silence between them grow fat and pregnant before Trevor announced he needed a break and set off toward the facilities shed.

"I know you saw something," Mac called out after him. "You know it too."

Trevor didn't look back. "I know it's time to eat lunch."

"You've got to deal with your demons. And you need to do it before they decide to deal with you first."

Trevor had no reply for that. Instead of eating in the shed, he took his sandwich toward what the college termed the "Reading Grove" but what Mac and Trevor privately called "Egghead Corner," a nest of shady oaks with benches where some of the more outdoorsy faculty liked to take their students when the weather turned mild. On such a hot day, Trevor expected to have the area to himself, but instead, he found a group of students sitting in a circle around a make-shift stage, an arrangement indicating the student literary club had decided to hold one of its poetry readings outside.

He hated those poetry readings, blaming them for causing him a week's worth of anxiety when he spent every day expecting to lose his job. It happened when Mac, during one of his better moods, suggested that the two of them crash one of these events during a break. Trevor had found it mostly boring, but the students seemed nice enough, and they didn't seem to mind them showing up to listen. The group consisted mostly of women, and as usual, Trevor wanted to avoid the creepy groundskeeper routine, so he felt self-conscious standing there in his sweaty work clothes. He even avoided eye contact when someone offered him a cup of the bitter tea they brewed for the event, offering a polite thank you and trying not to notice the remarks Mac made under his breath. *Do you dare me? I'll do it, just watch.* Sure enough, Mac did, even though Trevor didn't dare him. When the last speaker finished, Mac raised his hand and suggested that *he* take a turn on the stage and read everyone a poem he'd written. Naturally, those bright-eyed students wanted to show they were accepting of even the lowliest grounds worker, the salt of the earth, so they applauded with extra intensity to encourage Mac to make his way to the stage.

Mac prefaced his poem by saying, "This is a short poem about me." That made even Trevor curious, even if he knew whatever came out of Mac's mouth next could cause serious trouble.

And he didn't disappoint.

Mac's short poem, the one about himself, went like so:

Guns
Boobs
Motorcycles

Then he took a bow that lasted at least four seconds too long, enjoying what amounted to a smattering of polite but confused applause, far less encouraging than the first round.

Each day after that, Trevor expected the Dean or the Provost or whoever to call them in and fire them both for crashing a student-run event. But Mac kept telling him not to worry. "They loved it. They ain't complaining. My poem helped lighten the mood after all that heavy suicide shit they were reading."

"But it wasn't a poem. You stood up and said *boobs* to a bunch of girls who pay tuition here."

"At least I didn't say *tits*. That one might've crossed the line, but college girls love it when middle-aged guys like me say *boobs*. They hear their grandpops say it. I might've detected an interesting leer from one or two. But most of them think it's quaint."

"I don't think they do," Trevor said. "I really don't. And you don't even ride a motorcycle, so the poem's not even about you. I don't know where it came from."

"It came off a t-shirt, as a matter of fact. I saw some guy wearing it in line for Chinese take-out. It stuck with me. I thought it was funny."

"It'll really stick with you when they fire us."

"The girls won't talk. Trust me, they loved it."

To prepare her for his inevitable firing, Trevor described the incident to Madeline, including Mac's opinion about how charming the students found his use of the word *boobs*.

Madeline didn't exactly agree, but to Trevor's surprise, she didn't disagree either. Instead, she found the whole story funny and didn't see it as the road to ruin that Trevor believed it to be. "He's right about one thing—you really could lighten up a little."

Trevor didn't remember Mac say he needed to lighten up, but okay.

Madeline asked, "Is Mac married? Divorced? Gay?"

Trevor felt certain, or almost certain, that Mac wasn't gay. He hadn't confirmed his bachelorhood at this point. "I can't imagine anyone putting up with him long enough to be married to him," he said.

Madeline's expression changed, getting that faraway look in her eyes he knew too well. "We ought to be on the lookout for someone to hook him up with."

Trevor said, "I'd rather not."

But he said that about a lot of things, always backtracking somehow and doing them anyway, like his pledge not to go anywhere near any poetry readings happening in Egghead Corner. But there he stood under one of the oak trees, keeping a safe distance while eating his sandwich, his attention captured by a dark-haired student who read lines that sounded awfully familiar, though at first, he couldn't recall where he'd heard them:

Oh stay, three lives in one flea spare,
Where we almost, nay more than married are.
This flea is you and I, and this
Our marriage bed, and marriage temple is

And so on, going on for a few more lines with words full of strange images whose meaning eluded him. Still, the poem resonated with him, and before the poem concluded, it hit that it sounded an awful lot like that hymn or Bible verse or spell—no, *the poem*, he realized—that Madeline recited for him some time ago, though Madeline made some key changes, substituting a leech for a flea.

Lost in thought, his vision blurred as he tried to decipher the meaning behind it, and when he refocused, he realized the woman reading the poem had stopped speaking. She hadn't left the stage. Instead, she stood gazing at him as if hoping to catch his attention, to share a moment with him. The crowd didn't stir, though some of those gathered turned back to look at him, as if sensing something of significance in the air that didn't include them. Not that he noticed because he found himself experiencing an eerie moment of familiarity. Maybe his eyes just hadn't finished adjusting, or maybe the early seconds of heat stroke had kicked in. But it struck him that the woman who just finished reading this poem about the flea looked an awful lot like Madeline.

 EIGHT

As for Madeline, the *real* Madeline, she loomed at the center of the other strange thing that happened that day.

The shelf she rearranged had become a permanent altar of sorts to Little Lugosi, his plastic container a constant fixture between the two candles she kept lit, replacing them when they burned down too low. Trevor assumed she did this because leeches liked light, or something along those lines, but Madeline drew his attention to how the flickering illumination played upon the surface of the plastic, creating an ever-present aura around the leech. "A sacred effect for a sacred creature," she said.

For feedings, she continued to use her own blood, resulting in a series of angry red welts along her arms. *Hickeys*, she called them. At this point, Trevor managed to avoid having his own arm serve as the food source again—in fact, the welt left by the first time hadn't gone down, and it annoyed him constantly, often opening up in a fresh well of blood. Once, Mac even asked him if he'd visited the blood mobile recently, and Trevor had replied, "Yeah, that's it."

When he came home after hearing the flea poem, he found Madeline doing the strange thing he witnessed.

She stood before the altar, naked except for a pair of panties. Despite the shadows in the apartment, Trevor could see the gooseflesh on her arms, her nipples pert and erect. In one hand, she held the pencil she used to remove Little Lugosi from his feedings. On its tip, he wiggled with excitement, with something like ecstasy. He'd grown quite a bit too.

In her other hand, Madeline held a different object. It took Trevor a moment, but he soon recognized it as a blood-soaked tampon.

Trevor stood with his back to the doorway, watching as Little Lugosi squirmed at the end of the pencil, seeming to rear up, as if it could smell the bloody tampon. In just a short span of time, the leech had grown significantly, nearly doubling its size. Trevor noticed that Madeline maintained some distance between the leech and the tampon, as if she wanted it to bridge the short gap itself, as if she wanted to train it, wanted it to learn that it could extend its body toward its meal, with Madeline just there to coax it, to encourage it. Like a doting parent. Maybe like a lover.

And with Trevor there as a silent witness, it succeeded. It latched onto the tampon with lips or teeth or just a tongue—Trevor had no idea of its biology, but he would swear he could hear *sucking* sounds.

Madeline dropped the arm holding the pencil and focused on Little Lugosi, holding the tampon closer to her face, where a smile formed, a smile that didn't fall away when she turned and finally saw Trevor there witnessing every moment.

Then her gaze shifted downward toward Trevor's waist, where despite the fact he still wore his baggy work pants, a very visible erection had formed.

Soon enough, they went at it, him and Madeline and, he supposed, Little Lugosi, who floated happy and bloated in his little container, now placed by Madeline on the side table next to their bed. As he thrusted into Madeline's body, Trevor felt himself extend deeper inside her than he'd ever done before, each movement bringing him into contact with secret places in her body, sparking sensations that felt new and mysterious and exciting. During their lovemaking, he noticed that Little Lugosi began to swim joyously, wisps of blood swirling in the water around him, like a miniature ballet, a performance with tiny red flags. Their orgasms came simultaneously, resulting in a shuddering release that left Trevor breathless and exhausted. When he collapsed on the bed next to Madeline, he noticed that Little Lugosi's dance had ended as well, the creature seeming to have experienced its own release.

The silence hung heavy until Madeline finally broke it.

"That thing I told you I wanted to try."

Trevor nodded, his chest still rising and falling, great waves beating against him. He knew what she meant.

"That thing. Would you do it?" Madeline asked.

Put Little Lugosi on his cock. For some reason, neither of them wanted to say it out loud.

"I don't know," Trevor said, surprised at himself for not saying no immediately. He still hadn't returned to his body. "Maybe?"

"Think about it," she said. "And if the answer's no, that's okay. There are other things we can try too."

"Other things," Trevor repeated, not exactly asking a question. Below his waistline he could see smears of Madeline's menses covering his groin. Again, that wonderment at the female body, its network of tubes designed to expel, expel, expel and always be right, always be perfect and normal. *She wants me to bleed too*, he thought.

"More stuff happened at work," she said. "Don't even say it, I know what you're thinking. No, I'm not letting Little Lugosi feed on any more of the residents. Like I told you, Mr. Driscoll was special, his blood mixing with ours in Little Lugosi."

Deep inside his body, Trevor still throbbed. As he listened to Madeline, he reached out with his index finger and tapped the plastic container. Inside the water, Little Lugosi hugged the side of the container and seemed to throb with him.

"So what happened?" Trevor asked.

"I went through his things. Mr. Driscoll's things. When someone like him checks into that place, they just shove whatever personal belongings they have into a closet, and if they die and no family claims any of the stuff, they just get tossed into a box, maybe thrown out eventually. Who knows? Anyway, I found an old address book, the kind old people like to keep around, and wouldn't you know it, I came across a listing for Rose—right there under *R*."

The memory of that naked apparition came

back to him, and he suddenly felt cold as he thought of that grotesque leech-like thing hanging between its legs. His own body retracted as he recalled how that phantom walked into the bedroom. *Right here in this room*, he thought, *it spoke that name: Rose.*

Madeline said, "Remember what I told you about no surviving relatives? Well, I called the number anyway, and would you believe I reached a church? Before you say anything, I know, not a good sign, but the woman who answered? It was Rose. Not dead after all. She works there or something. It doesn't sound like a big church, probably the kind that meets in one of those lonely, abandoned-looking strip malls. Anyway, I'm going there Sunday. Mainly to meet her."

"Mainly to meet her." Trevor repeated those words to see if saying them out loud would help him understand. He withdrew his finger from the plastic containing Little Lugosi, and in turn, the tiny creature let go and began floating freely, as if to meditate on the meaning of the universe or the existence of God.

Madeline said, "I'm not going for any religious

reason. Just to talk to her about her grandfather. I mean, he died alone, without family. I was the closest thing to a family member he had. Trevor, you need to understand; that's hard sometimes. There's nothing worse than dying alone, all by yourself."

"You bringing that?" Trevor meant Little Lugosi.

"*Him*. Am I bringing *him*, you mean. No. Or, I mean, I don't think so."

Inside the dresser, they kept a pack of smokes. Seldom did they touch the cigarettes, and by now, the pack must've gone stale, but Madeline reached for one and lit it. She offered one to Trevor and he took it. They lay on the bed smoking. *So stereotypical*, thought Trevor, *a cigarette after sex*. He thought of offering one to Little Lugosi.

Then Madeline said, "I won't bring him if you go with me. That's what I wanted to know. If you'd come along."

"I don't think so." The taste of the cigarette nearly made him gag. They *had* gone stale.

"I'm not good around new people. And it could

be fun. Maybe they speak in tongues. Wouldn't that be fab?"

He managed to remain noncommittal all week, planning to find an excuse at the last minute if he needed to. Little Lugosi continued to grow, and twice more Trevor caught Madeline feeding him with a tampon. Like the first time, the sight of that act aroused him and it led to more fucking, even more furiously than last time. Bloodier too. Though never one to keep track of Madeline's menstrual cycle, it seemed as though her period had gone on and on interminably. Her body simply didn't want to stop bleeding.

NINE

Trevor managed to keep evading the question of whether he'd go with her to meet this Rose. He felt no desire to go to that church, or any church for that matter, but he maintained such a constant state of arousal around Madeline it became almost impossible to say those words. He felt light-headed all the time now.

Growing larger and larger, Little Lugosi seemed to thrive on Madeline's menses, nourished by the period that would never end. In a strange way, that period nourished Trevor as well, flooding his senses in ways he'd never experienced. She smelled different. She tasted different. He breathed her in at every opportunity and relished burying his face between her thighs, growing high from her fragrance and coming up for air in a blood-drunk stupor.

Still, he didn't want to go to that church with her and meet some stranger named Rose.

The perfect excuse to skip out on Sunday came from Mac, who called Saturday evening, telling him he absolutely needed to come to the campus the following morning. "I've got something to show you," Mac said, sounding almost giddy about it.

"Just tell me what it is. I don't like these games."

"Just be there. You don't want to miss this." With that, Mac hung up.

Mac said the same thing earlier that week, convincing Trevor to meet him at a bar after work, using that same, "You don't want to miss this" line, and Trevor fell for it. On that earlier occasion, he showed up and met Professor Cleveland Barnswallow.

Former Professor, it turned out, because when Mac promised academic help with the pig problem, the anthropology or archeology professor he referred to had actually lost his position at the college some time ago. That explained why Trevor didn't recognize him.

"An indiscretion," the former professor said as he shook Trevor's hand. "A stupid indiscretion, in fact. You can't imagine the sort of pressures that an academic must face, especially when confronted by nubile young women, all desperate to curry favor so they can earn a higher grade."

"You don't say," said Trevor, who didn't want to know.

"I do indeed. In this very bar, in fact. Had I not agreed to meet a certain young woman here, I would still be gainfully employed by that wretched institution. Now I spend much of my time here. Alone."

Former Professor Barnswallow didn't look capable of seducing a young college student. Middle-aged with a protruding belly, a shiny bald head, and a very round, red hairless face, he looked like a giant baby. He smelled faintly of mothballs and licorice. Evidently, he could sense Trevor's thoughts.

"Don't let my appearance deceive you. I'm quite irresistible to young women," he said.

"You don't say," Trevor said again, and once more former Professor Barnswallow answered with an "I do." But all preliminary talk ended when Mac called them over to a table he'd secured on the far side of the room, well away from the little activity the bar saw at that early hour.

The real conversation started when Mac said, "Trevor here saw the Minister."

The former professor showed no immediate reaction. He took the first of a series of bold sips of the brown liquid that filled his glass.

"I see," he said as he wiped his mouth with his wrist. "A rare sighting. What I wouldn't give for a sighting of the infamous Minister. Mac, you of course know that I have my doubts as to the existence of this animal."

Mac didn't look discouraged at all. "But you don't *not* believe in it either."

"Oh, I know there's a basis in fact. Though my actual specialization is sociology, collecting stories about the Minister became a hobby of mine. History isn't my official bailiwick, however, and when I made it known that I planned to publish an article about the Minister and what his significance is to Vissaria County, it just so happened that my little indiscretion took place. A coincidence the administration took as an opportunity to end my tenure? I think not. Mac, my drink has gone dry already. Would you mind replenishing it? You know this information already."

Mac grumbled, but he took the empty glass to the bar.

With small eyes buried in a mound of red baby flesh, the former professor regarded Trevor. "He's a delightful man," said Barnswallow.

"He has his moments. I mean, basically he's a good guy. Just a little …"

"Obsessed? Perhaps he needs the Minister to alleviate a tedious job."

"It's not that tedious."

"Not with the pigs constantly tearing up the landscape? I imagine that still happens."

Trevor thought about asking the former

professor if he knew why Mac behaved so strangely around rabbits, acting almost afraid of them, but before he could put the thought into words, Mac came back with a new glass filled to the rim. Barnswallow accepted it gratefully and took an enthusiastic gulp, causing nearly half of it to vanish immediately. Mac sat down with an elbow on the table. "What'd I miss?" he asked.

"Just talking about the pigs," said Trevor. "We did go out in the woods a few days ago."

"Quite the swathe of wilderness around that campus," the former professor said. "A very ancient forest, you know. Unlike the rest of our state, hurricanes have passed through this area only rarely, so what you see there has been left to grow undisturbed for centuries. And it must've been quite a trek. Those acres of wilderness do stretch for miles, don't they?"

"Yeah, that they do. And about what Mac was saying: we split up, and I just got a little overheated. Mac found me by what's left of some old building out there."

Barnswallow's eyes seemed to twinkle as he

listened, as if he relished knowing something no one else knew.

Trevor continued: "I don't remember walking there. I was near a pond, where I might've seen a pig, and … well, I'm not sure."

"A pond, you say?" Barnswallow's demeanor changed. "You found a pond? Not *the* pond. My goodness, if you mean the pond I'm thinking of, what luck! Gentlemen, I've searched high and low for that pond during my employment at that infernal institution, and would you believe I never could find it?"

Trevor looked at Mac, then back to Barnswallow, worried suddenly that he'd said too much. "It's pretty well-hidden inside a hollow. But it's there."

"Amazing," said the former professor. "Simply amazing. And you say you found yourself amongst some ruins?" That twinkle again.

"Yeah, just a bunch of rubble around an old foundation."

Mac added: "He looked out of his mind."

"Well, see here, the pond and that old building

are linked. I know about the ruins. I found them myself on one occasion, and after recording their location, I urged the provost of the college, that old prune, to have them marked and preserved as a historical site of some importance. Not that she'd listen. She just wanted to talk about my indiscretion."

"Linked how?" asked Trevor, not wanting to hear any more grievances about that *indiscretion*.

After draining more from his glass, Barnswallow said, "By time and event. You see, that old foundation belonged to a church, an extinct one, I might add, with some rather eccentric practices thankfully lost to time. The congregation used to hold its baptisms in the waters of that pond, and they were interesting ceremonies, to say the least. At the time of these baptisms, the pond was, by all accounts, rather large. Apparently, it's retracted over the decades, and when I could never find it, I'd assumed that it dried up completely. What an astounding find you made! Tell me, could you retrace your steps and locate it again?"

Images of what transpired that day near

the pond flashed through Trevor's mind. That enormous pig, practically as large as a tractor, and its grotesquely swollen tool. He never told anyone about it, especially given the awful coitus he interrupted. That woman, naked and running into the trees, out of his field of vision. He felt certain, or at least almost certain, that it wasn't Madeline and that he imagined the whole thing.

The former professor's question hung in the air. Mac looked at Trevor as if wondering if he'd ever get around to answering. Finally, Mac answered for him. "We can find it again. I mean, it ought to be pretty simple. We're smarter than we look. Ain't that right, Trevor?"

"Why does it matter?" Trevor practically shouted, hoping to hide his distress. That elicited an expression of amusement on Barnswallow's face, as if Trevor ought to already know the answer. Trevor's arm began to itch and bleed. He did his best to hide the marks from the other two. Just recently, he'd once more let Madeline use his arm in another feeding for Little Lugosi.

"Because of the extraordinary nature of those

waters—assuming the old accounts turn out to be true. Apparently, the pond is home to a particular breed of leech that grows to an unusual size, and it wasn't uncommon to find them as large as thirteen inches in length—sometimes even larger than that. These creatures served as an integral part of the baptism ritual. You've heard of snake handlers, I assume? Or snake cults? Well, the flock of this church became drawn to that particular spot because of the leeches. The baptisms took place with all the participants in the nude so that their bodies would be fully exposed to the leeches—to attract them. A baptism, of course, normally means being washed of sin. To have the leeches feed on one's body signified something much greater than the purification of the body. When one submerged oneself, the hope was to come back to the surface as covered with leeches as possible. They regarded it as a blessing."

Hearing all this brought forth a fresh wave of irritation on Trevor's arm. He did everything he could to resist scratching it. From his pocket, he took out the stale pack of cigarettes that he and

Madeline once kept by the bed. He lit up and offered one to Mac. Mac accepted, but after his first drag, he gave Trevor a look and stubbed it out.

"It must have appeared quite the scene," Barnswallow continued. "The practices no doubt appeared pagan, un-Christian, even blasphemous. Not what a good, pious soul would expect from a ceremony honoring the so-called savior. In truth, it's not clear what sort of god this church worshipped. Perhaps they worshipped the leeches themselves. But oh, they did love their baptisms. Can you imagine it? Coming up with your body covered in a squirming mass of black bodies, all of them feeding on your blood? The pain would cause religious ecstasy. Visions even. Soon they dropped the pretense that their ceremonies had anything to do with purification or redemption. Only the visions mattered. I'd give anything to know what they saw. Would you look at that, Mac? My drink has gone dry again."

Mac paid for a refill, though not without some grumbling. Even Trevor wanted to hear more, but the former professor wouldn't continue until his glass came back replenished. The more he drank, the more he *did* resemble a giant baby.

When Mac sat down again, Trevor prompted him before he could begin demolishing his new drink: "You said they were like snake handlers."

"Oh, yes, indeed. Did I already mention that the leeches there grew quite large?" Trevor and Mac nodded at the same time. "Well, they could become quite monstrous, in fact. Perhaps because of the frequent feedings proffered by the worshippers. To their minds, the leeches were endowed with supernatural powers, and the largest ones would be carried to the church for other ceremonies. According to the accounts, it took two men to carry the largest one. Quite unimaginable, really, and likely exaggerated. Or perhaps they caught some sort of eel. In any case, these other ceremonies proved even more blasphemous and obscene than the baptisms, and the rumor mill became quite active. Just imagine the lascivious things one can do with a leech."

He paused as if Mac or Trevor might want to share an idea or two. When neither of them spoke, he took a thirsty gulp and went on. "It didn't take long for some of the church's more outspoken critics to form a committee to investigate. And by that, I mean, of course, they formed a mob. At first, they made a stealthy approach, sneaking up to windows to see if the rumors were true. What they saw shocked and angered them. What angered them precisely, I can't say. The blasphemy perhaps? The evidence before their eyes that the members of this congregation worshipped the leeches and not the holy father? Perhaps that alone couldn't have spurred them to act as they did. Some returned from the scene muttering about some kind of birth, the emergence of something that required swift and decisive action. Gentlemen, I am the only one drinking."

"Just go on," Mac said. "Tell us what they did."

"It was a slaughter," Barnswallow said. "A massacre carried out under a setting sun. Inside those ruins you stumbled upon. A mob of justice seekers, but really just prudish bigots. Using axes, machetes, even farm equipment, they murdered everyone in that house of worship, including their leader, a very charismatic gentleman who apparently fathered several children inside that congregation. They saved him for last, using horses to draw and quarter him. Once they finished this massacre, they burned the church and left the bodies there to rot. For days, they left their handiwork there to stew in the sun, until someone with a guilty conscience decided to return to the scene of the crime, perhaps to give the victims a proper burial. Instead, this person found a gaggle of wild pigs, a sounder of swine feasting on the remains."

"The Minister," said Mac, sounding far away.

Barnswallow nodded. "The Minister."

"Wait," said Trevor. "What?"

"The spirits of those people live on in the pigs," said Mac. "They became meaner. More unruly. And the Minister is called 'the Minister' because—"

Barnswallow finished for him. "Because he ate the head and torso of their charismatic leader. That's why he's called the Minister. The leader of that unorthodox church lives on inside that animal.

You've heard it has a special fondness for human flesh. At one time, there was even a police detective who swore that the animal ate his leg. At least that poor fellow survived, and much of the Minister's notoriety stems from that man's account. As for the Minster's other victims, they weren't lucky enough to walk—or at least hobble—away."

TEN

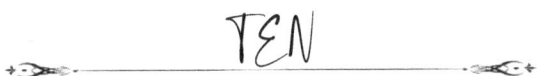

Allowed to go uninterrupted, that talk would have extended well into the late hours. It became obvious that former Professor Barnswallow liked to jaw, and he certainly liked the way Mac kept buying him drinks, so they got to hear the same story a second time, though in a less artful, less coherent way. They eventually abandoned Barnswallow, leaving him in sole possession of the table, badly slurring even as he continued to babble to himself.

For that reason, when the second plea came from Mac to drop everything and come join him as soon as possible, Trevor would've ignored it if not for an overwhelming desire to get out of

Madeline's church plans.

She didn't appreciate it. "I don't like going to new places by myself."

"Then don't go," said Trevor.

The welts left by Little Lugosi continued to irritate Trevor, and he scratched them constantly. Madeline had a lot more of those spots than he did. He wondered how she could stand it. He never saw her scratching madly like he did.

"I'm going," she said. She wore the yellow dress that Trevor loved for the way it accentuated her hips. As happened numerous times that week, he felt a deep ache for her growing inside him. It required a conscious effort to keep his hands off of her. "I promised Rose—and I genuinely want to meet her. Come on, Trevor, don't be an asshole. Come along with me."

Underneath that dress, Trevor knew, a tampon continued to absorb the blood from a period that simply wouldn't end. The smell of it permeated everything—her hair, her skin, her clothes. It intoxicated him, making him perpetually aroused. He practically needed to steady himself before he could answer. "I just can't. Mac needs me. There's some kind of job to do."

"On a Sunday. You're going to work on a Sunday."

"The pigs don't stop eating on Sunday."

The lameness of his own excuse made him wince. Like he could give a shit what day the pigs chose to fuck up the landscaping. He just hoped he wouldn't find former Professor Barnswallow waiting with Mac. Before leaving, he regarded the altar for Little Lugosi, where two new candles sat burning. Inside the container, the leech continued to grow big and fat. Trevor wondered when it would outgrow its home, especially if he gave any validity to Barnswallow's story. The thought made him afraid.

Things started off in a promising way when he found Mac waiting for him alone, striking that cowboy pose of his while leaning against his truck. No former professor in sight.

"You don't look so good," Mac said.

"That's funny. I feel great. Never better." The marks on Trevor's arm started bleeding, and without thinking about it he used his fingers to wipe the blood away. He put his fingers in his mouth to lick them clean and immediately thought of Madeline in that dress.

Not really caring how Trevor felt, Mac grinned. "You need to see what I did. I finally bagged the fucker. It's done."

He led Trevor across more chewed-up grass toward the facilities shed. A rabbit lay in their path, a particularly brave one judging by its still presence. Maybe it learned from past experience that Mac posed no threat to it. Even now, Trevor noticed the great lengths Mac went to circle around the animal, giving it plenty of distance. He didn't understand this thing about Mac and rabbits. Good thing the Minister wasn't a rabbit.

"Bagged the Minister, you mean," Trevor said to fill the quiet.

"Sure as fucking shit. I spent the good part of Saturday on the hunt, and just as I was about to pack it in, I made one more pass by those church ruins, and there he was. Just looking at me with the most evil look an animal can muster."

They reached the facilities shed, and even before Mac rolled open the door, Trevor smelled something rotting and dead.

"You keeping him in there?"

"Where else was I going to put him? I wasn't going to leave him out there. You need to see it."

The metal wheels on the door screeched as Mac rolled them open. In the midst of disordered landscaping tools, wedged between a mower and the far wall, sat an unfamiliar table made of worn wood, something large covered by a tarp. Normally, Mac hardly ever smiled, but he did so much of it now that Trevor thought it might warrant re-naming him Mr. Sunshine. He waved Trevor inside, where the smell grew even worse, especially as he approached the table. The bloody bumps on Trevor's arms itched and bled miserably the closer he came to the covered form. Once more, he licked his fingers and felt his crotch stir.

Mac said, "Drumroll, please," stretching the last syllable like a carnival barker. Then he gripped the edge of the tarp, and with a flourish and a flick of the wrist, he snapped it away.

Trevor stared at the animal uncovered before him. At first, it appeared as if the black hide of the animal moved, creating the illusion that it continued to draw breath. Then Trevor realized that an assemblage of live black leeches remained rooted to its stomach.

"That's it, isn't?" Mac asked, still wearing the grin that looked so alien on him. "What you saw. What got you all turned around in your head. Told you I bagged it."

A gaping hole marked the animal's side, the result of the weapon Mac used to kill it. More black creatures writhed around that hole, some burrowing their way into the pig. Tiny white ones too. Maggots, Trevor realized. One of the leeches fell off and hit the floor. Mac crushed it with the heel of his boot. It popped like a balloon filled with blood.

Trevor said, "Yeah, you bagged it all right." But on that day near the pond, he saw a different creature. The pig he saw in the act of coitus with the woman looked significantly larger than this one, practically the size of a small horse. He couldn't imagine the other pig even fitting on the table. It had a darker hide too. This one on the table looked more dark-brown than black. Trevor walked around the table to study it more closely, trying to hide the revulsion the leeches stirred inside him. Another one fell onto the floor, and when Trevor looked down, he saw the ground had become littered with the small bodies, all crushed like the one he saw Mac stomp. Trevor also saw a much more modest-sized tool between the pig's legs, nothing like the stalk he saw dangling from the other pig. The tusks of this animal looked different too—yellowish white, nothing like the unnatural black he saw on its enormous cousin.

While Trevor studied the carcass, Mac opened the small refrigerator they kept in the shed. Officially, it was meant for their lunches, but they maintained a supply of beer inside it too. Mac pulled out two cans, giving one to Trevor. They clinked the bottoms of the cans together.

"Cheers, brother," Mac said, and they drank.

Stifling a burp with his wrist, Mac's eyes narrowed. "You don't think it's him, do you?"

Trevor regarded the dead animal, noticing how some of what he took as leeches looked more like worms. They continued to fall out of the pig's body, and he helped Mac step on a few of them.

"No, I don't," Trevor finally said. "I want it to be, but I don't think it's him."

Mac burped again. Then he said, "I dreamed this moment, you and me standing here like this. You doubting the truth before us. In my dream, you said those exact words: *I don't think it's him*. So you know what I did?"

Mac held up a finger to delay Trevor's answer, going to the tool bench and returning with something in his hand. Trevor stiffened when he saw what Mac held: a long, serrated knife.

"Before I tell you what I did, here's what else happened in my dream. You kept arguing that we needed to restore the pig to life. On account of its innocence, you said. You said we needed to re-animate this pig because it was a mortal sin to kill an innocent creature like this. Don't ask me how you planned to do it. You just said you knew the secrets of re-animation, and I believed you. So I said, *For the sake of all that's holy, for the benefit of all mankind, we must consign this spawn of darkness to hellfire.* And to prove to you that it *was* the Minister, I cut its gut open and out spilled human remains— eyeballs, fingers, arms, even a leg still wearing a cop's shoe. Plus, a head. Your wife's head. In my dream, you picked up the head and started crying. *My Madeline*, you said, *fouled by this terrible beast.* I know, neither one of us talks that way. But only by suffering that pain of recognition could you understand the rightness of what I did. And then you helped me burn the carcass. Trevor, my man, how is Madeline these days?"

"What?"

"I say, how is Madeline?"

"She's fine. Never better. At church."

"That's a good place to be. Don't think me a cold person for asking the way I did. I just want to check and make sure you know where she is before I do this."

Mac positioned the blade against the pig's stomach.

"You going to cut it open here?" Trevor asked.

"You and me," said Mac. "We're like those two fellas in the shark movie, the ones who snuck onto the dock and cut that big old fish open." That smile again, his teeth big and white. It made him look insane. "Let's see what's inside it."

With a quickness Trevor didn't know his co-worker possessed, Mac cut into the animal. Using the serrated edge, he began sawing, the grin still fixed to his face. The rancid smell grew stronger, and the flies buzzed angrily as the dead thing's insides began to spill onto the table and the floor.

Trevor covered his mouth and nose. His task complete, Mac stood next to him.

The gutting revealed no human remains. Only glistening, wet organs, and thousands of worms, an untold number of maggots mixed in with their number, all squirming on the floor now, too many to stomp to death. Trevor breathed through his mouth and willed himself not to vomit.

"Those guys in the movie," Trevor said, "didn't they find an old license plate or something? The way I remember it, they had the wrong animal too."

ELEVEN

They managed to drag the pig's carcass into the bordering woods, having planned to return for picks and shovels so that they could bury it. But the whole task of moving it proved so back-breaking, they didn't have the energy for any digging, so they elected to leave it under a tree and let the vultures do their work.

"You could carve it up. Bring home bacon for Madeline," Mac said, wiping away sweat. He leaned against a tree and breathed hard.

"I don't think so. All those worms? The fucker's diseased."

"You said that right, partner. Plus, I keep forgetting your lady's a vegetarian. What's the saying? *Happy wife, happy life.* That's in the Bible, you know."

Trevor left Mac there to gather his breath and went back for the plastic trash bag they used to stuff the spilled guts into. When Trevor came back, he threw the bag next to the pig. As for the squirming mass of worms on the floor of the shed, they decided to leave that for the next day. Tomorrow, they'd shovel them out, and with any luck, they'd just crawl away or burrow beneath the earth before that time came. Trevor didn't feel hopeful, though. He kept thinking he should've just gone with Madeline to meet this Rose, endure whatever church service that meant suffering through.

Happy wife, happy life. Though no scholar, Trevor felt pretty certain that saying didn't come from the Bible.

Madeline told him the name of the church at some point, though he didn't know if he remembered it correctly. *Vissaria Church of the Unredeemed,* or some such shit. That didn't sound a good name for a church.

The name came to mind as he dragged himself

back inside the apartment. Pain shot through his back as he pulled off his boots and studied the slimy, crushed bodies on the soles. Some of the bodies belonged to crushed leeches, some still writhing.

Unredeemed. That didn't sound like a healthy state of mind.

The silence of the apartment amplified unpleasant connections to Barnswallow's story. Worse, he felt a headache begin to uncoil, first making its intentions known by tapping on the inside of his skull. *I'm gonna start pounding soon*, said the headache. *Tap, tap, tap.*

It took a moment to realize he heard actual tapping.

From somewhere inside the apartment.

Tap, tap, tap.

A funny impression formed that the tapping came from the vicinity of Madeline's shrine to Little Lugosi, as if he'd heard the leech itself tapping to him from the inside of its plastic container. There it went again, *tap, tap, tap,* three times in quick succession, just like before, so he had to go over and look.

As he approached, the headache uncoiled further, as if it intended to push aside everything else in his head to make room for itself. When Trevor looked at the altar, he saw two red candles left burning, not much more than nubs now. Between them sat the container with Little Lugosi's name on it filled with water. And nothing else.

Part of Trevor really believed he'd see the little creature inside tapping for his attention.

He thought, *It's empty now because the little fucker's crawled inside my head, and he's tapping there instead.*

He should've felt happy. Elated, really, because she finally got rid of it. Flushed it, hopefully, before it became so large that it clogged up the commode. According to former Professor Barnswallow, they could actually grow that large. A vision formed, a man with shirtsleeves rolled to his elbows, standing before the congregation of a pioneer-era church, his arms outstretched. Squirming black bodies clutched in both fists—not snakes, but a mass of leeches, grown to monstrous sizes. Bruises and welts marked the skin of his arms from where they'd fed. Blood too. From his mouth issued a gospel of sorts, just not the sort of old-time gospel one might expect.

Trevor rubbed his temples, trying to rid himself of both the headache and this image.

The sight of the empty container inspired dread instead of relief. He didn't know why. It occurred to him he might be coming down with an illness, like maybe the flu. Didn't pigs carry strains of the flu that could be passed on to humans? He didn't know for sure. Or maybe letting that leech feed on him resulted in some kind of disease, perhaps passed on from the dying Mr. Driscoll.

The urge to lie down and sleep came over him.

Madeline might say he needed some time with Little Lugosi feeding on him to balance his humors. That would help him recover, she'd probably say.

His breathing grew heavy, but he quickly fell into sleep. Once, he awoke, and not finding Madeline, he reached for his phone and sent her a text. He didn't know if he successfully composed the message, but he did hit *Send.* He just wanted to know where she was and why she hadn't come home yet. Each time he awoke, the light appeared different, and he couldn't tell how much time had passed—minutes, hours, days? Not even dreams to give him a clue about time, not that they would prove reliable. In dreams, a whole lifetime could go by in a single minute.

He finally did dream, though. The details felt very real. The dream started with more tapping, the same kind he heard when he returned to the apartment. This time, the tapping came from someone knocking on the bedroom door, and for a moment, he convinced himself he was awake and this was no dream at all. In fact, he assumed the knocking came from Madeline, who'd finally come home, and he very much wanted to see her. It felt like he hadn't seen her in so long. Why had he even closed the bedroom door? So of course, he called out to her to come in.

But the form that stepped into the room didn't belong to Madeline, and he returned to his original theory he was dreaming. He hoped he was dreaming because he had no desire to see the naked back of the old man who entered instead of his wife, an old man with a curved spine and skin covered with sores and age spots. He entered the room with his face turned away from Trevor, and he carefully closed the door behind himself, as if courteously trying not to awaken its sleeping occupant.

I am not awake, Trevor told himself, even though he felt very awake.

He watched the hunched form shuffle its feet toward the foot of the bed. Then without a sound, it turned and looked at Trevor, as if presenting its body for study.

Like the last time, most of its body lay in shadow, but Trevor saw all too clearly the thing between its legs. A black mass, squirming and pulsing. Feeding. A leech covered the man's genitalia, feeding on him. It looked as though this specter, this phantom, this dream had positioned itself in a precise way so Trevor could gaze upon it.

An awful thought occurred to him as he watched this display. He knew Madeline had let Little Lugosi feed upon Mr. Driscoll before he died. Had she done it this way? It reminded him of what she fantasized about doing with him. What he, on some level, desired himself.

The Driscoll-specter held still as Trevor watched, the only movement occurring with the thing between its legs.

More tapping broke the stillness. It turned into pounding. Someone else at the door now, and not tapping politely but demanding immediate entrance.

That elicited a horrible change in the phantom. It smiled, revealing a toothless mouth. Then it spoke, a cracking voice, as if long disuse had made speech difficult.

"He wants in," it said. "Are you ready to admit him?"

Trevor didn't want to answer. To answer would mean acknowledging the reality of the thing before him, and to hear his own voice might prove it wasn't a dream. But somehow, the phantom heard his unspoken answer. "Your child. Your savior," it said, answering the question he wanted to ask.

That made no sense. He had no child, certainly no savior. Once more the phantom seemed to interpret him without speech.

"You do. Or you will." The knock again, louder, more demanding, as if something on the other side intended to break down the door. "You'd better answer. No miracle should go unacknowledged. No blessing without sacrifice."

More pounding. The walls shook.

"Answer!" The phantom's scratchy voice rose to a piercing shriek that made even the leech pulsing at its groin jump in surprise.

But Trevor couldn't move, a paralysis resulting either from his dream state (he desperately wanted it to be a dream) or from his unwillingness to move, his fear of what would meet him on the other side of the door. When he remained still, the phantom sighed.

"Your child has no arms. It can't enter on its own."

Another hard knock, and Trevor heard the sound of cracking wood. The naked phantom made its way to the door, resigned to doing the work itself. Trevor followed it with his eyes. Echoes of splintering wood filled the room. Nevertheless, the door seemed to hold. As it took the doorknob in its hand, the phantom turned and seemed to regard Trevor with sadness. Then it opened the door.

Trevor squeezed his eyes closed. He didn't want to see what came into the room, this *child* of his. "Behold," the specter said, but Trevor refused, though he could sense it slouching about the room, shifting furniture violently as if seeking him out in a fit of blind anger. Eventually, Trevor felt its weight on the bed with him.

Involuntarily, he opened his eyes then, only briefly, but long enough for a glimpse of its sleek form.

It appeared as if a velvet cape covered it from head to toe, and for an instant, Trevor thought about the day the leech arrived in the mail and the inspiration for Madeline's choice of a name. She said it shared the name of an actor who played Dracula, and it did in fact appear caped and sinister. During that short moment when his eyes opened, Trevor also noticed the sheen of what now shared the bed with him, how it seemed to glisten with moisture, how it pulsed, as if fat on blood. As it made its way further up the blankets to nuzzle against him, Trevor tried to call out for Madeline. But he couldn't, and somehow, the effort exhausted him. In this dream, for it had to be a dream, everything eventually went blank, as if he'd fallen into the deeper sleep of death.

TWELVE

"Hey, here he is."

The voice ruptured the darkness. He stirred, realizing he'd sweated through the sheets. As she leaned over him, he felt her weight pressing down on the mattress, her breath warm in his face.

"You don't look so good, Cowboy."

Madeline used to call him that all the time. *Cowboy*. Still afraid he might see the slouching thing, Trevor parted his eyes only slightly, just enough to gaze into the face leaning over his. Fog seemed to overlap her features, much like the fog that filled the hollow the day he saw the Minister. Her lips formed into a familiar half-smile, the one that always made his knees turn to jelly, starting back from the day they first met. *Hey, Cowboy*. She started with that, and from that moment on, he belonged to her.

But the next time Madeline spoke, her voice came from far away, and somehow, she did so without even moving her lips. "He's in there? For fuck's sake, he should be at work."

He tried to talk, but couldn't do so, his throat too sore. He wanted to ask her how she managed that trick, speaking without moving her lips and sounding so far away. Instead, he just coughed. A lot came up, including blood. From far off, he heard a toilet flush. Madeline continued to smile down upon him.

"Don't come in here," she said. Her lips moved this time, and she sounded closer. She meant these words for whoever flushed the toilet. The other voice—*her* other voice—replied, the words too muffled for him to hear clearly. Then she spoke again. "He's got it. The flu, I mean." The face hanging over him continued to regard him with a half-smile. Something looked different about it now. Too arch, he realized, and also it didn't smell like her. He knew then this face didn't belong to Madeline at all, even if it looked so much like her. "The swine flu, I bet. You absolutely cannot catch this, Mads. Not in your condition."

Mads. Madeline liked it when her friends called her that, but Trevor loved the sound of her full name. At first, she told him to call her Mads like everyone else, but he kept falling back into Madeline, and she decided she liked the sound of her name when he said it. Madeline. He wanted to say it now, but the effort led to more coughing.

But it didn't matter. He realized this woman leaning over him wasn't even Madeline. He'd seen her that day in the Reading Grove, Egghead Corner. The recognition must've shown on his face because she nodded.

"Yeah, we've met, Cowboy. You heard me read that poem. I thought we shared a moment there, but you ran off. I know you can hardly talk, can barely even sit up. The flu hit you hard. But I'm here to take care of you. I'll take care of both of you. I'm Rose."

More coughing in reply. Rose helped him sit

up, and he expelled gray mucous that left his hand wet and sticky. He felt her hand pat his back as he continued to expel the contents of his lungs. The coughs wracked his body. They hurt so much he hardly noticed when the pats on his back became caresses.

Apparently, Madeline said something from the other room. Rose said, "I got him. We're becoming fast friends already. You really need to stay put out there. Think about your condition."

"Condition?" Trevor managed to say.

But Rose ignored the question, her head cocked slightly, eyes askance, listening to a reply that Trevor couldn't hear.

Then she looked into his face and said, "You call in sick, Trevor?"

"What day is it?" he asked. To his own ears he sounded like the ghost of Mr. Driscoll, just air blowing through a lifeless body. "What condition?" He didn't want Rose in the room with him. He wanted Madeline.

"It's Wednesday. Mads kept trying to reach you, but your phone was turned off. She shouldn't be traveling around like this, but we started to worry about you. No one's heard from you. I told her I should check on you alone, but she insisted on coming along. Good thing I checked the bedroom before she did. You don't want to expose her to what you have in her condition."

"What fucking condition?" he managed to ask.

"Trevor? Mads is pregnant. You're going to be a dad."

THIRTEEN

That made no fucking sense. In a fevered rush of words, he explained why. To this Rose, this stranger who looked inexplicably like Madeline, he told her in a strained voice about all the blood, about the period that wouldn't end. He even told her about the passion it kindled in him, how just the scent of her body stoked a desire that at times became virtually unbearable. He talked and talked, not sure what he was saying much of the time, the sweat of his own fever getting into his eyes so that her face became a blur as she nodded and smiled at his words. But she didn't seem to understand.

"That's love. Beautiful love," she said. "I'd love to share it with the two of you. And now she's pregnant. You know that happens, right? And she loves you so much. Right outside this door, I have her all set up on the sofa. She wants to come in here to see you so badly, but both of us know she can't do that. This flu you have, it's bad. It could kill the baby."

But the period that wouldn't end. Once more he mentioned that. Soberly, she regarded the bloodstains on the sheets that Trevor pointed out.

She said, "Looks to me like you've been coughing up blood."

"Not me," said Trevor, his voice hoarse.

"I'll clean these up later. I'll be here for a while. For you both." Then that half-smile again, so much like Madeline's.

"Stop smiling," Trevor said. "That's not your smile."

"Rest," she said, smiling.

"You don't know us. Where's Madeline?" He called her name as loud as he could, but it came out sounding like a femur caught in a garbage disposal.

"Trevor?" Madeline's voice came from the

other room, sounding so distant, a thousand miles away. "Rose, what's wrong with him?"

"Fever's not broken yet," Rose said.

Trevor started to get up. His old friend the headache resumed its work, and he suddenly vomited and fell back onto the bed. He tried to get up again and found himself covered in his own sick.

"I can't take care of you," said Rose, "if you won't listen to me. Mads?"

"Yeah?" Trevor heard her voice more clearly now, and he started to call back until Rose produced a wet rag and began cleaning his face. A sour taste filled his mouth, and he gagged.

"Tell Trevor to listen to me," said Rose as she wiped away the sick. "Tell him it's in his interest and especially yours."

"Listen to Rose," called Madeline. "She's here to help us."

Once more, Trevor tried to sit up, and to hold him in place, Rose straddled him. Through her clothes, he could feel the heat of her body. With her weight, she held him down as she wiped away the rest of the vomit. He fought against her, but her strength proved too much for him.

As she worked on him, she asked, "What'd you do to the door?" She asked this question as if she already knew. "The wood's cracked. Looks like someone tried to cave it in with their fists." Her thighs squeezed around him, and he felt her knees press into his ribs. "You're not the kind of guy who likes to use his fists—or are you?"

"I don't know what you're talking about." The last word came out as a squawk as she increased the pressure on his ribs, cutting off his air.

"Remember," said Rose, "that Mads is in a delicate condition. Can't have you going around using your fists in any old way you like. You need to understand the door's staying closed. You're not going to try to bust it down, are you?"

How could he tell her about what *did* happen, about that wet, glistening thing banging on the door until Mr. Driscoll let it in so it could slouch around the room and eventually climb into bed with him.

Positioned in much the same way Rose was

now.

Did that really happen, the banging and the cracking wood?

She squeezed him even more and pressed down on his chest at the same time, causing him to call out in pain.

From the other room came Madeline's voice. "Is that Trevor? Is he okay?"

"Just feverish," Rose said. "Along with some aches and pains." Then more quietly so that only he could hear, "Do you like me this way? Mads says you like it when she does this. Do you like me this way too?"

"No," he croaked. But then she did something even worse. She took off her shirt, exposing her pale, bare breasts. Grabbing his wrists, she positioned his hands upon them. As he struggled to pull them away, he squeezed reflexively, causing an unexpectant spurt of milk to shoot from one of the nipples. It struck him in the face, getting into his mouth. It tasted all at once sweet and coppery.

That prompted her to laugh aloud. "Oops," she said. She reached again for the rag she used for the vomit and began cleaning his face again. "That's not supposed to keep happening." Leaning close so her lips came within a few inches of his ear, she asked, "Did you like that? Or would you rather see me another way? On all fours, maybe? My ass in the air? Do you want me to be your little piggy?"

She leaned back to gauge his reaction.

Winded, he managed to ask, "What do you want?"

"To take care of you, Mads, and your little piglet. I owe Mads, you know, for what she did for my grandpa. Did you ever meet him?"

Perhaps he hesitated too long before he shook his head. Her half-smile returned as she studied his face.

She said, "He raised me in that church, you know. The Church of the Unredeemed. He taught me to love my body, to respect my body for its natural functions. Not to hide them out of some fear of sin. He taught us to sanctify ourselves through our own blood. But when he started going soft in the head, we had to put him away, and pretty soon, everyone else started to die off or move away. Now it's just me keeping it going in a fucking strip mall, right in between a Dollar Store and a Radio Shack. But I've kept it going, preserving everything I could, all the pictures, the documents, the history. I was the only thing keeping it from dying out—until Mads came along. I showed everything to her, and she got it immediately. She understood. More importantly, I understood *her*. We connected immediately. You know, there are things she can't talk to you about. Life and death things. Birth things. When she came to meet me, we talked all the way into the night and even into the morning. When she finally fell asleep, I kept her warm and safe. And now, I'm doing the same for you." She touched his forehead and frowned. "Well, you're keeping yourself warm all on your own, but you get my meaning."

A knock interrupted her speech. Simultaneously, their heads turned toward the door. A moment ago, Trevor wanted nothing more than for Madeline to come into the room, but if she did that now, she'd see Rose straddling him with her iron thighs and leaking breasts.

But Madeline didn't come inside the room. Only her voice did. "You promise he's doing okay?"

"He'll be fine, but you need to lie back down. Don't come in here, Mads, I mean it. You don't want this flu, I promise you."

"Madeline," said Trevor, "call Mac for me." He said this because his phone had disappeared, probably taken by this insane person on top of him. "Tell him I need to see him."

"Depends on whether or not he's had the swine flu," said Rose. "Me, I've had it, and it's no picnic, trust me, but I should be immune by now." Then she leaned closer to Trevor's face. A drop of her milk fell onto his lips as she said more quietly, "You wouldn't *believe* how I got the swine flu."

FOURTEEN

The door continued to separate them, Trevor falling in and out of sleep, wakened intermittently by Rose, who brought him bowls of greenish soup she forced into his mouth. He struggled to keep it down, and several times he soiled himself. At one point, he awakened to discover she'd outfitted him with some kind of adult diaper. Waves of delirium washed over him as he observed her with detached curiosity cleaning him with a sponge and basin of water, humming some discordant tune as she paid an inordinate amount of attention to his groin. Through unfocused vision, he could see she'd stripped herself naked to carry out such tasks. "You're pretty filthy," she said, "disgusting,

115

actually. Can you believe your body produced all this?" But she didn't sound disgusted at all, more amused than anything, and she concluded these sessions by covering him with her own flesh, which made his temperature spike even further. *She's trying to kill me*, he thought.

Eventually, he awoke to a different face, and at first, he attributed it to one of the frenzied dreams that plagued him. The face belonged to Mac, and he blinked the sleep from his eyes to see if the face would go away, but it remained and came into further focus. Rose, dressed for now, loomed over Mac's shoulder, watching.

"Trevor, my man, you like shit. And I ain't saying that to be mean. You actually look pale."

Trevor could tell from the concerned expression that Mac said this without exaggeration.

His first attempt at a reply failed, and Mac's lip curled in disgust as Trevor coughed up a glob of something green in color, probably undigested soup.

"You shouldn't be here," Rose said, eyes still on Trevor even though she spoke to Mac, "he's pretty contagious."

"I ain't never been sick a day in my life," Mac said without looking at her. "Okay, just once. After we cut all the worms out of that animal, I had the runs like you wouldn't believe, but that went away. Looks like something hit you bad."

"Madeline," Trevor managed to say, "where is she?"

"She's out there. I just saw her, Trevor. I thought I was your friend."

Trevor studied the genuine look of hurt on Mac's face.

"We are friends," Trevor said. "Partners."

"Well, why didn't you tell me you're expecting? Or I mean Madeline's expecting." He looked at Rose now. "Ain't that what you're supposed to say when a fella's wife is in a family way? You say they're both expecting?"

Rose shrugged. She watched Trevor.

"Anyhow, you could've told me. Partners, we are, just like you said. I thought you'd tell me something like that. All this time and not a word."

"She's not pregnant," Trevor said. "She can't

be." He started talking about the period that wouldn't end, but he kept coughing and the words came out garbled.

"He's been like that," said Rose. "You ought to let him rest."

But Mac ignored her. "Trevor! Get your head right! You're going to be daddy. I just saw her. Stomach's out to here. But she doesn't look so hot either. I'm worried about both of you."

"I'm taking care of them both," Rose said.

"You got your work cut out for you."

"He's more difficult, obviously. Mads is perfectly fine. Just pregnant."

That word brought the hurt back into Mac's voice. "And you didn't even tell me. I'd tell you if I were going to be a daddy. That's what friends do. They share things."

"Go on, Trevor. Share something so Mac can leave," said Rose. "Before you get him sick."

Mac thumped his chest. "Iron constitution. Never been sick in my life, so I'm not afraid of no flu. It should be afraid of me."

"Rabbits," Trevor found himself saying, "he's

118

afraid of rabbits."

Neither replied right away. Her arms folded across her chest, Rose regarded him with curiosity. Mac glowered at him, the hurt gone away, replaced by something that looked like betrayal.

"You avoid the rabbits," said Trevor. He didn't know what point he intended to make. It just seemed important to say it. "You're afraid of them."

"I'm doing penance," Mac said. "It's my burden."

"Penance?" said Rose. "To rabbits? What the fuck?"

"Rabbits hide, and they leave their young where you can't see them. Especially when you're riding one of those big old mowers we use at the college."

That held everyone in silence, and for a moment, Trevor forgot about himself and about Madeline. He stared at Mac, still absorbing the implication even as Rose spoke it out loud.

"Holy shit. You rode over a litter of bunnies with your lawn mower?"

"It's called a *warren*," Mac said. "As I said, I must do penance, and when the rabbits come upon me now, they do so with the understanding that I will do no harm to them or their spawn."

Her arms still folded, Rose shook her head and laughed. But Mac didn't seem to notice. To Trevor he said, "But I told you that before, and now you're making me say it again in front of a stranger."

"You never told me." But Trevor wondered about all the times he tuned out this man's nonsense, and he wondered if he simply hadn't heard.

"I did, but you didn't even tell me that *you're expecting*."

"I tell you, she's *not*."

"He's delirious," Rose said, "and you're making him worse. You should get out of here. You catch what he has, you'll be sorry."

"Madeline isn't well," said Trevor. "She's not safe, Mac. From her. She's a witch or something."

"I'm not the one who put the cracks in the door. You see what he did over there?" Madeline asked Mac.

120

Mac nodded. "Busted up. I saw. Trevor, you trying to put your fist through the door?"

"Get Madeline out of here. She needs to get out of this apartment."

"He's right about that," Rose said. "She does need to get out for some exercise. I'm planning on doing that soon. Have her do some walking. In her condition, she needs that."

Mac patted Trevor's leg, making sure not to touch any of the soiled areas of the sheets. "You hear that, partner? Rose is going to get her out."

"You do it," said Trevor. "Get her somewhere away from here."

Mac laughed. "Where would I take her? To work with me? Show her the facilities shed? We still got worms in there, you know."

"There's some nice walking in the woods around there," said Rose. "I was thinking of taking her there, actually."

Mac turned and looked at her, his expression becoming critical. *There*, thought Trevor, *he finally sees there's something wrong.*

Mac said, "I've seen you out there, haven't I?

You a student?"

"Not right now. But I come out there sometimes."

"You go to Egghead Corner, don't you?"

"What's Egghead Corner?"

"Where the Eggheads go to read poetry."

Without a trace of sincerity, Rose laughed and touched Mac's shoulder, like he'd just told a good one. Rose said, "Yeah, I go out there and listen sometimes. I mainly come out to tell people about my church."

"A church girl," Mac said.

"She's a witch," Trevor said, but they ignored him.

"Yeah, I'm a church girl. Maybe I can come out and talk to you about it sometime."

"Don't," said Trevor, but he began to cough. Mac recoiled at what Trevor expelled from his lungs. Rose insinuated herself between them and started pouring something milky white into a medicine cup.

"You need to go," she said as she began forcing the liquid into Trevor's mouth. "His humors, they're all out of balance. They're making him delirious. In the old days, a doctor would've come to bleed him." Mac didn't leave right away. "Go!" she said.

Mac apparently responded to the command in her voice because when Trevor managed to see through his stinging tears, he no longer saw his friend, and he began to feel very sleepy. *Some kind of narcotic*, he thought, *she gave me a narcotic. Something she's excreting herself*, he imagined in a wave of dizziness, and for the umpteenth time, he fell into a deep slumber.

FIFTEEN

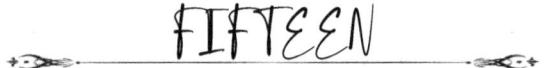

Air moved sluggishly in the room, just enough to cause the blinds to move and allow the flickers of an afternoon sun to penetrate his eyelids. As he bordered upon waking, the light made him think of the midway where he met Madeline for the first time. The time she called him *Cowboy*.

Hey, Cowboy. I need someone to ride with, she said to him at the Vissaria County Fair, the one that arrived every fall, and she'd called to him from the Wipeout ride. She sat alone in one of the cars, the attendant moving in the opposite direction with his back turned, still taking tickets and seating other riders. At first, Trevor didn't realize she meant him. He stood by himself near the metal barricade to the ride. *Me?* He mouthed the word while pointing at his chest, to which she nodded furiously, time ticking by, the attendant sure to turn at any moment to see her encouraging Trevor to jump the line and hop in. *Hurry up,* she said, *jump over the gate and get in—I'm not riding this thing by myself.* He hesitated. He'd come to the fair alone, having pinched a free pass at a drugstore counter and not having anything better to do with himself that day. *Jump the fence NOW,* she whisper-yelled, *before that asshole sees you.*

Then she gave him that half-smile that made all of his hesitation go away. It worked like a spell. Trevor hopped over the fence, a rare athletic feat for him, and he settled in beside her before the asshole attendant had time to see anything. Together, they rode the Wipeout, the centrifugal force of the ride pushing her up against him, their shoulders crushing together and the two of them laughing at the whole exploit. Before the ride finished, they knew each other's name.

Trevor never did anything like that before, something so impulsive. They spent the rest of the afternoon and the evening that followed at the fair together. Trevor found out Madeline's boyfriend broke-up with her barely an hour before she called Trevor over to hop the fence. No mourning the break-up for her. She decided she never liked the bastard anyway, so good riddance. And why should she have a day at the fair ruined by someone not smart enough to realize she was a catch? She told Trevor all about it as they rode the carousel together.

Later, as the moon came out, they shared their first kiss at the tallest point of the Ferris Wheel. As they made their way to the bottom, Trevor knew he never wanted the ride to end, never wanted to leave her presence, to always bathe in the glow that seemed to surround her. For that reason, he found himself agreeing when she said she wanted to find the Freak tent.

Still, he had to say something. *I don't think they have those anymore.* But she kept insisting. There had to be a Freak tent, what kind of carnival didn't? So together they explored the outer fringes of the fairgrounds, eventually finding a ride isolated from all the rest, a haunted house, as it turned out, one you experienced by riding through it in a tiny car barely big enough for one adult. But they squeezed in together, Madeline and Trevor, holding hands now as if they'd known each other forever, and once more, their shoulders pressed together as the doors to the haunted house swung open and the car took them inside.

Mostly empty darkness inside, occasional cobwebs hanging in their faces and deep, sonorous laughter piped in through hidden speakers. Just as Trevor found himself reaching the conclusion the ride contained nothing scary at all, something finally happened, right before the ride reached its finale. It proved quite a climax to a lot of nothing.

A real person—or so it looked to Trevor like a real person—lurched out of the shadows toward them without any of the stuttering motion one would associate with the crude animatronic figures found in such rides. An actual person, a woman. *Help me!* she screamed, wearing what looked like the remains of an old prom dress. Even in the dim lighting, the blood covering her neck and shoulders looked startling real. *Help me!* She screamed again in a voice that didn't sound like a stage voice, instead one that conveyed genuine pain and terror. As the car rolled past her, Trevor could see two things: one, her left breast was exposed, not at all the kind of thing he expected at a kid-friendly fair, and two, another figure lurked in the shadows behind her, one cloaked in a black cape. From the folds of the cape extended a pale hand with sharp, overlong fingernails, threatening to grasp the woman, about to pull her back into the shadows.

But before the scene could conclude, they found themselves back outside, breathless at what they'd seen. Already the safety bar of the car had begun to rise, and the attendant, an old man in coveralls, began ordering them to disembark. *Was that real?* Trevor asked Madeline as they stumbled away. *That couldn't be real, could it?* But Madeline laughed at his reaction. *That was amazing*, she said, and still intent on finding a Freak tent, she led him past the ride. Beyond the haunted house, they came across RVs and old cars that looked past their time of operation, along with a garbage barrel someone used to create a low-burning fire.

Next to the barrel sat a woman wearing a Tupac shirt and smoking a cigarette who regarded the two of them with a dour expression. They intended to steer clear of her, respecting her privacy; she surprised them by waving them over to her and offering to tell their fortunes.

Madeline couldn't resist. Her hand in Trevor's felt hot and sweaty, and he didn't mind that in the least as she led him to the woman. On a TV dinner tray that held her ashtray, the woman dealt out a series of cards, and by the firelight, Trevor saw the symbols they contained: cups, wands, swords, and one bearing the picture of a man suspended upside down. The last one remained face-down, and after a monotoned expression of the card's meanings, the woman explained the final card would tell them their destiny. With a flourish, she flipped the card. Its face revealed a man and a woman in an embrace. *The Lovers*, said the fortune-teller, her tone still flat. *Your destiny is together*. Somehow, by this point, Trevor already knew this fact. Judging by the way she gripped Trevor's hand, Madeline knew it too, and with their arms around each other, they handed the woman a twenty and began walking away.

Wait, the fortune-teller called to them before they made it very far. *There's a card in the dirt. A jumper. It fell from the deck. You need to pay attention to this one.*

They returned to the woman's tray table to see the new card the woman placed next to the others. On it, they saw a grotesque creature who had bound the lovers to him with chains. *The Devil*, the woman said as she drew upon a new cigarette. The flames of the fire danced in her face as she regarded Trevor seriously. *You'll need to protect her. If you love her, promise to protect her. Protect each other. Promise now.*

They promised in front of the fortune-teller, and that became the first way they ever expressed their love for each other, though neither one used that word, not yet. They wouldn't after all, not even knowing each other for a complete day yet, but they still felt the truth in their promises.

Madeline promised, and Trevor promised. Later, they could tell themselves it all amounted to a joke, a performance in front of this woman who seemed to believe in the message of the cards and treated it as such a dire warning. Yet the promises turned into something much greater.

Until now, he'd hardly remembered those promises, but now, as he roused himself from the slumber of the flu, he thought of how he made his. Stubbornly, his eyelids opened, and he looked about the room. Empty now—no Rose, no ghosts, no leech pounding at the door. Just the sound of his own breathing and the reek of his illness. Remarkably, he felt fine now, no longer sick, but as he struggled out of bed and tried to make his legs remember how to work, he found the whole apartment empty. No candles burned now on the altar, and the container had fallen over, leaving a stain of rancid water on the wall and floor below. On the couch nearby, a bundle of used blankets and a pillow that still bore the imprint of Madeline's head. A glass half-filled with water. An unfinished bowl of that stomach-turning soup.

Everyone had left, but his intuition told him where they'd gone and where he must go now if he wanted to fulfill his vow to Madeline.

SIXTEEN

As if sensing something in the air that day, the campus had gone quiet, the exodus of students having begun early, perhaps in anticipation of some holiday Trevor couldn't remember. Whatever the case, the absence of activity made it easy to spot Mac's truck sitting near the path that led to the facilities shed. Though he moved sluggishly and his legs felt cramped, Trevor felt a swell of energy when he saw it sitting there. He wanted and needed Mac's help.

As he limped up the path, he saw the pigs had continued to wage their destruction in his absence, and Mac apparently couldn't keep up with the onslaught on his own. His eyes scanned the trees for any sign of life, human or animal, and when he saw none, he picked up his pace.

He hoped when he opened the shed, he'd find the three of them waiting there. Madeline ready for the kind of embrace he longed to give her for what felt like weeks. Mac ready to accept the declaration that Trevor loved him like a brother, never mind how stuck up and conceited he might have seemed tin the past. And Rose.

Rose. He still didn't fully understand where she came from or how she'd so easily insinuated herself into their lives, but they needed to set boundaries for her because whatever care she gave Madeline during those awful past days when he fell sick hadn't done her any good—that much he knew, especially if she looked as bad as Mac described. Plus, those delusions about pregnancy, they didn't need that either. It sounded so unhealthy, just another obstacle for them to overcome, much like Little Lugosi, whose absence from the apartment gave Trevor the hope for a fresh start. Perhaps when Trevor opened the shed door, he'd find Mac with his rifle trained on Rose, holding her in check until Trevor's heroic appearance, at which point they could summon the proper authorities. Not that Trevor knew exactly what laws she might have broken. Something, he assumed. Or he hoped.

But when he rolled up the metal door, he saw only the table on which they'd gutted the dead pig, its grain still covered in dried blood.

The ground below it still writhed with the worms that fell from its belly, the only life the shed held.

That made Trevor think of the knife Mac used to cut the pig open. He looked for it, the bodies of the worms and maggots squishing under his feet. But he couldn't find it, nor did he know precisely for what purpose he wanted it.

Outside, he finally found himself in the presence of someone else, just not someone he expected to find: former Professor Cleveland Barnswallow.

"Well, I'll be dashed. This is an unexpected pleasure," said Barnswallow. "Are you here for the expedition?"

The former professor wore tight-fitting khaki

shorts and a matching shirt, along with a baseball cap with flaps hanging over his ears and neck. The beads of sweat on his face made him gleam like a red beacon. His smile made him even brighter, so that Trevor practically had to squint. As before, he thought of a giant baby.

"Expedition?"

"The expedition to find the pond. Mac promised me an expedition once the holiday began."

Once more, Trevor considered the absence of life on the campus. "Holiday?"

"Why, Thanksgiving, naturally! You know, of course, that I cannot show myself on this campus during normal business hours. The provost, that crusty old labia, set firm ground rules when my dismissal came. All because of that imbroglio I told you about, the minor indiscretion. So of course, we had to wait for a holiday." Then he noticed Trevor's condition for the first time. For once, Barnswallow said something in a voice that Trevor didn't consider yelling. "What happened to you? My god, you look awful. Your eyes are redder than

Mars."

"I've had the flu."

Instinctively, Barnswallow backed away.

"I'm okay now," said Trevor. "Where's Mac?"

"You don't know? I thought of the two of you as joined at the hip, the two working-class comrades, eager to buy a disgraced academic like me drinks for evening. He said he'd meet me here."

Once more, Trevor studied the tree-line in the distance. Barnswallow's eyes followed his.

"He started ahead of us, do you think?" Barnswallow asked.

Trevor took a deep breath as he debated how much he ought to tell the former professor. When he could come to no resolution, he took a deep breath and set off toward the path that led into the woods. Overhead, the sun had begun to make its descent, setting the trees afire with orange light. Behind him, he heard the sounds of the former professor attempting to catch up with him, mumbling a string of words Trevor couldn't decipher other than *expedition*.

But he knew he couldn't let Barnswallow

distract him or slow him down. Instead, he needed to move quickly, to clear his head so his intuition and memory could lead him and help him retrace the steps he made on the day he fell into that mental fugue. Even with the thinning light, the temperature seemed to rise the further into the woods he went. Despite the approaching Thanksgiving holiday, it felt unseasonably hot.

Though gasping for air, Barnswallow continued to keep pace with him, his ongoing mumbling increasingly becoming incoherent babble.

Behind him, Barnswallow barked something.

"What?" Trevor asked without turning.

"I said, is this really the way? Are we going much farther?"

Trevor didn't know what to say. Maybe he needed Barnswallow with him on this trek. After all, he seemed to have some kind of special knowledge, given what he said about the leech-handlers and their rituals. Such a repugnant thought, but now he felt certain that Rose belonged to that religion—*cult*, he corrected himself—and that she intended to carry on its practices with Madeline. If she'd convinced Madeline that she'd somehow become pregnant—once again, impossible considering the period that would never end—then she must have some kind of lurid purpose in bringing her to this place. Maybe Rose hoped that the hidden spots in these woods held memories of what those people once did, and bringing Madeline out here would reawaken them, bring them to light. The thought chilled him.

But no thought unsettled him more than that of the Minister, that gigantic animal, so majestically black, still fattened on the remains of the body it consumed so many years ago. Trevor now decided he believed in the Minister, its existence undeniable. He had seen it. He saw it couple with Rose, no more resisting the truth in what he'd witnessed. And now he felt certain she had something similar in mind for Madeline, who in all likelihood had no idea what lay in store for her.

Yes, he needed Barnswallow to help him make sense of these events, to help him explain them to Madeline if necessary. His words alone wouldn't suffice. Behind him, the former professor stopped to lean against a tree. Breathing heavily, the man took a flask from his pocket and began drinking its contents.

"No time for that," Trevor said, still forging ahead. "Move!"

More grumbling from Barnswallow, but he returned the flask to his pocket and set off after him. "Is this the way?" he asked in a voice that sounded winded.

"Yes."

But as Trevor moved on through the wild brush, he struggled to recollect the path he'd taken that day after splitting up with Mac.

No use asking Barnswallow. He'd never found the pond on his own, and he couldn't help Trevor now.

What if, Trevor thought, they both wound up lost and directionless?

That day at the fair came back to him again, how he thought occasionally of the bloody woman who appeared at the end of the haunted house. At various times, he'd almost brought her up with Madeline and asked her if they should have hesitated before moving on. They could've asked the attendant: *Is there supposed to be a real woman inside there? If not, we saw one, and she might be hurt.*

But maybe only *Trevor* saw her and Madeline failed to notice her entirely. If so, then the responsibility lay squarely on his shoulders, and he had to live with the possibility the carnival ride contained some real psychopath who actually hurt, maybe even murdered, an innocent woman. At the time, it proved easier to dismiss it as just part of the show. Yet the doubt remained, and in retrospect, he felt the gravity of his inaction, his fear of appearing a fool who was easily frightened by carnival tricks. He ought to have said something. He knew that now.

Finally, a clearing appeared ahead, but not the hollow with the pond as he anticipated. Instead, a slight rise revealed the old church ruins. In the dried grass, something lay in a heap. A rabbit hopped on top of it, as if to draw Trevor's attention towards it. His breath quickened as he moved closer, with the former professor not far behind but clearly struggling to keep up, his breath hot on the back of Trevor's neck.

"God's bones," Barnswallow said as they got closer and the heap came into focus. "Is that—?"

It was.

As Trevor drew nearer, he saw more rabbits. To avoid looking at the heap, he tried to count the rabbits, stopping when he reached twenty. They'd gathered around the heap but parted to make way for Trevor's approach.

Amongst the rubble and decay lay Mac's body. Together, they stared at it.

"Look at that. Something's devoured him," the former professor said from over Trevor's shoulder. He seemed to want to keep Trevor between himself and the remains, Mac's abdomen now a gaping maw with intestines dangling from the cavity, his organs glistening red and purple in the sun's golden rays. A rabbit hopped across the former professor's feet, causing him to lurch back. "The rabbits? They did this?"

Trevor had to choke back a sob before answering. "No." He forced himself to study the carnage. Something had indeed feasted on Mac's body, sizable chunks bitten away and regurgitated in the surrounding grass. Nearby sat a pile of feces—human or animal in origin, Trevor couldn't say.

"He was such a delightful man," Barnswallow said, sounding close to tears. "Who would do such a thing?"

Trevor didn't answer, but he had his ideas. The main cut in the body looked linear and uniform, calling to mind how Mac slit open the dead pig in the shed. This cut looked nearly identical. Above that, Mac's eyes stared ahead blankly, his mouth hanging open as if in the middle of voicing a complaint. Elsewhere, Trevor could see what might have cut off that complaint: an open wound in the neck, a twin to the one in the abdomen. Trevor hoped Mac went quickly.

One of the nearby rabbits stood on its haunches, clearly sensing something. It looked to the west, and Trevor followed its gaze to where the woods thickened. Apparently, Barnswallow looked too, because once again, he spoke first.

"It's him," he said, no longer sounding like he wanted to sob. "Just look—he's amazing."

There stood the monstrous pig, its tusks as black as its hide, its eyes small and red. Its form commanded the landscape, and though the two of them stood in frozen awe, the rabbits surrounding Mac's body began to scatter and hide. The pig dominated Barnswallow's attention to such an extent that he seemed to not notice the other thing Trevor saw.

Just behind the pig stood a form that looked human. Mostly human, at least, the body naked and female, but the neck leading to the head of a pig. The head looked badly decayed, its fur falling away in places to reveal bone. It took Trevor a moment to identify it, but even at that distance, he could see the body belonged to Rose, while the pig's head looked like it came from the butchered animal he and Mac once carted off into the woods.

The sight held Trevor spellbound until Barnswallow finally saw the woman.

"Oh my," said the former professor, his voice barely above a hush. He sounded vaguely aroused, which would have offended Trevor if he didn't feel that way too. Despite the death around him. Despite everything, including himself.

Before he could answer Barnswallow, Rose turned and disappeared into the trees, running as swiftly as he saw that day near the pond. The Minister took the time to blow a huff of air to show his contempt for them before he turned as well and followed her.

"After them!" the former professor said, but Trevor didn't need any encouragement. He'd already started in their direction.

SEVENTEEN

The pair wanted them to follow, Trevor sensed. Seldom did he lose complete sight of them, and even then, he could detect where they'd gone based on the sounds of disturbed brush and breaking branches. Despite the heft of his weight, Barnswallow kept pace with Trevor, the sound of his labored breathing never far behind.

The chase would end at the pond of leeches. Trevor didn't just hope so, he *knew* it, just as he also knew that in that place, he'd find Madeline. He just didn't know in what state he'd find her. The lingering uncertainty motivated him to overcome the complaints in his limbs, sore from days of disuse and hunger. For Madeline, he kept running, not for the nakedness of Mad Rose with her pig head nor the chance of seeing the Minster again. All for Madeline.

Without warning, the ground dipped, and he tumbled rather than ran into the hollow. When he managed to get himself upright, he saw it.

The pond, larger than he remembered, and another naked form on its edge.

Not Rose this time, but Madeline. Rose had disappeared from view, as had the Minister.

Trevor didn't bother getting to his feet, instead scooting and crab-crawling toward her. Behind him, the former professor found the hollow too. Trevor heard the other man gasp as Trevor made his way to where Madeline sat hunched in a strange position, her knees in the air.

As he got closer, he saw how terrible she looked. Even in the waning sun, he could see the blotchy rashes on her pale skin, her hair looking ragged and thin and missing in some places, her cheekbones caving into her face. Her stomach looked bloated, and until he saw her shudder, Trevor feared she'd died in the position she held, half-sitting, half-squatting, her knees apart.

Somehow, despite looking unaccustomed to strenuous physical activity, the former professor managed the uneven terrain much better than Trevor had. Unlike Trevor, he remained on his feet and slowly followed his path to Madeline before coming to an abrupt stop. On a rise to their left came movement, and Trevor heard the other man mutter his words with awe and surprise. "It's you, isn't it? I know you."

Trevor looked, fearing he'd see the Minister about to charge them, but instead he saw Rose again, still adorned with the head of the dead pig. In her hand, she held a knife Trevor recognized, the one from the facilities shed Mac used to gut the pig. The same knife, Trevor knew, that eventually ended Mac's life.

Her real face somewhere inside the skull of that thing, Rose still managed to speak in a voice they could hear and understand. The sound came to them resonant, amplified, terrifying.

"Hi, professor. It's me." She curtsied, a gesture made all the more grotesque from the blood and dirt that covered her.

Barnswallow gulped audibly. "What've you done?"

"You're not proud of me? Your little piggy?"

"An indiscretion. A small one," said Barnswallow, perhaps imagining behind one of the surrounding trees, the provost might be hiding and listening.

"Am I not your little piggy anymore? Or is this not scholarly enough?"

"You—" Then Barnswallow finally lost his footing. He slid down the embankment on his ample backside until he stopped within a few feet of Trevor and Madeline, his eyes still on Rose.

Before he could adjust himself to a sitting position, Rose came running. From inside the pig's head, she emitted a sound of wild rage. As she ran, holding the knife in the air, Trevor wondered how she could even see. It turned out she could see just fine because she brought the knife down just as she reached the prone, for once-speechless Barnswallow. The blade of the knife ripped into his stomach.

Trevor wanted to help the other man, but Madeline needed him, and he had to do something before Rose could turn her fury upon him.

Screams filled the air, Rose's and Barnswallow's, as Rose brought down the knife three more times into the former professor's gut. On the last strike, she kept it planted and began sawing down to his groin. Barnswallow's arms moved as if wading the waters of an invisible river, the volume of his voice thinning out to a wail as his stomach opened into a chasm wide enough for Rose to reach into with her arms. Instead of using the knife, she used her hands.

Trevor didn't watch the rest. Instead, he focused on Madeline, who seemed intent upon moving the whole of her naked body into the pond, her feet already in the water up to the ankles. She kept her knees parted, resisting Trevor's efforts to make her stand. She acted like she wanted to submerge herself, and Trevor could only assume she did so out of a desire to create distance between herself and the carnage on the shore.

Once more, he saw her distended belly as

he tried another tactic, grasping her under her armpits in order to pull her away from the pond. He managed to pull her back just far enough to see leeches now occupied the portions of her body once covered by water.

"No!" she shouted. The sound and volume of the command reduced everything around them to silence.

Involuntarily, Trevor stopped pulling and stared at her. Barnswallow's death-rattle abruptly ended, along with the wet sounds of his dissection. With his insides splayed out on the surrounding earth, the former professor no longer breathed. Trevor felt Rose's gaze watching him, watching Madeline, and that spurred him to stand. He got into the water with Madeline and once more tried to pull her to her feet.

Again, Madeline shouted for him to stop, and once more, he relented, if only briefly. He felt the pond's leeches latching on to the skin of his ankles.

At his feet, with a grimace of pain forming, Madeline let out a yowl. She spread her legs wider, releasing a ribbon of blood into the water that lapped between her legs, the normal pinkness of her cunt was an angry ridge of dark welts.

Behind her, Rose now sat on her haunches, no longer wearing the pig's head. It lay near her feet, its empty eye sockets glaring at Trevor. Rose's own eyes moved wildly between Trevor and Madeline, her breathing heavy. In both hands, she held two clumps of Barnswallow's guts as if she meant to compare their weights.

"Don't touch her," Rose said.

Trevor held still, meeting her gaze.

"What'd you do to her?" he asked.

The question made Rose smile. Not the half-smile from earlier, but one that showed all her teeth. No more chance of confusing her with Madeline. She picked up the knife and started moving toward them.

"Stay away," Trevor said. He shifted position, positioning himself in front of Madeline, who maintained her place in the water. He wrapped his arms around her, hoping to keep her shielded. On his hands and wrists, he saw the tiny forms of leeches.

Again, those words from Rose, louder and shriller. "Don't touch her!"

Half in the water, Trevor closed his eyes, knowing he would feel the knife soon. He waited for it, hoping to shield Madeline from its impact. The muck below them seemed to shake, ripples forming in the water as Rose brought her fury closer to him.

But he heard something else. A thrashing from afar, closing the distance quickly.

The violence he braced himself for never reached him. Instead, something else thundered out of the surrounding brush, and Rose let out a yelp of surprise and pain.

Turning, he saw the enormous black frame of the Minister on top of Rose, a reversed parody of the crude coupling he witnessed that day when he stumbled on the hollow alone. The Minister's shape obliterated nearly all sight of Rose as it tore into her with tusks and teeth. The sounds Rose made rose higher in pitch, sounds no one could mistake for pleasure.

Trevor couldn't bring himself to look away.

During one awful pause, the Minister's eye found Trevor's, and once more, he thought of the impression Mac shared with him some time ago— that a malevolent intelligence swelled within that animal, something almost human. Trevor felt it as they held each other's gaze. With its unblinking eye, the Minster demanded that Trevor worship it, seeming to bask in his awe and terror. When Trevor finally looked away, the Minister returned to Rose and ended her screams with the loud crunching of bone.

When Trevor looked again, he saw the creature had mangled her into wreckage of blood and ruined flesh. It had eaten her face.

The Minister stepped away from its meal and took two steps toward Trevor and Madeline. Rose's blood covered its black tusks, and bits of her flesh hung from its muzzle. Once more, it looked at Trevor, a question in its eyes.

Will you worship me?

The wrong answer, Trevor knew, would bring its wrath upon himself.

But not on Madeline.

154

With its presence, the Minister indicated He would stand guardian over Madeline, who had become indentured to Him, her role to serve some purpose in obeisance to Him.

Trevor still lived so he could offer the Minister his worship and that same obeisance.

"Yes," Trevor said out loud.

The Minister huffed, and despite the humidity, His breath was visible in the air. He didn't move, His absolute stillness both terrible and spectacular.

"Yes," Trevor said again.

Finally, the Minister moved, though not far. He would give Trevor the space he needed to help Madeline, but if necessary, He could turn and reach them in a matter of seconds. He showed that already with Rose. The Minister moved His bowels, leaving a rancid pile of shit for Trevor to smell.

But Madeline needed him.

More blood trailed from between her legs, and during the silent communication of the last few seconds, she'd moved further into the water so that more leeches now clung to her arms. Strain showed on her face, her beautiful wasted face, as she continued to push. The proximity of the Minister caused her no distraction. If she noticed him at all, she seemed to not care, nor had she registered what He'd done to Rose.

She reached for Trevor and gripped his hand, squeezing hard enough to cause pain. He thought she wanted help getting to her feet, but when he tried to lift, she stopped him.

"I need to ... get this out of me."

On the shore, the Minister moved closer to them, His attention once more on Trevor. Trevor relaxed his muscles and left Madeline in her position. Her naked abdomen, bloated and red, revealed more welts and the writhing bodies of other leeches. More of them latched on to Trevor too, but they seemed to cause him no pain now, though his head felt light and his vision began to swim.

"Inside me," she said, but a wave of pain caused her jaw to clench, and she couldn't say more.

There was just enough clarity in the water

for Trevor to see between her legs. She pushed, forming another ribbon of blood. But Trevor saw something else where her labia parted: a protruding black nub.

"What's inside you?" he asked, though he knew already what lay coiled inside her.

"Help. Me. Get. It. Out," she said between gasps. "It's killing me. Rose was wrong, so fucking wrong."

Trevor stared. At some point, either he'd let go of Madeline or she let go of him. Now he felt afraid to touch her, of doing something that might hurt her. He looked at what remained of Rose's body. He wanted to kick apart what remained intact. Eventually, he might feel pity for her. But not now.

"I don't know what to do," he said.

He looked all around, like he might find someone who could help. The Minister had moved farther away, now munching on something He'd dug up from the earth. Closer lay the gutted body of Barnswallow, dead because of him. Nearby, Trevor could see the knife Rose used.

They were alone. He was alone.

Did he need the knife to help Madeline extract the thing inside her? He knew he'd wind up killing her, if not from any cuts he made, then from the infection that would come afterwards. Besides, he sensed if he made any attempt to take the knife, the Minister would react.

Beside him, Madeline made a sound.

"Tell me what to do," he said.

She strained, her skin turning purple. Her voice, when she spoke again, came out in a hoarse whisper. Through half-lidded eyes she looked at him. "Reach in and pull it out."

Once again, he looked down and saw more of the blood-fattened thing emerging from her vulva. Its sheen glimmered in the water as it wiggled.

"I can't," said Trevor. The sight of it made him sick.

"Do it," she said, even weaker now. "I can't push anymore."

So Trevor reached into the water, finding its slickness difficult to grasp. It wiggled even more as if sensing a predator. It wanted to stay where it was.

"It won't let me," Trevor said.

Fading fast, Madeline used what remained of her strength to grab his wrist. She squeezed, forcing him to look her in the eyes, and there Trevor saw all the love she felt for him, tender love that told him to love her back meant overcoming his revulsion and doing this one last thing for her. She moved his hand back between her legs. "Reach in," she said. "I'm going to push hard. One last time. With everything I've got."

He nodded and began working his fingertips in between her wall of skin and the slippery form lodged within her. At that moment, he felt it latch on to his skin, and a dull pain began to throb from his fingertips to his elbow. The world seemed to tilt at that moment, the landscape going sideways, and he struggled to maintain his balance.

"One. Two. Three," Madeline said. Then her face bunched up as she gave that final push.

With a sucking sound, Little Lugosi came free. Trevor stumbled back a step or two as it finally emerged into his arms, as if recognizing the taste of his blood and having absorbed everything it

159

could from the tissues of Madeline's body, it now chose to continue its feast on him instead.

The leech had grown considerably inside Madeline, its girth fat and its length astonishing to behold. Madeline convulsed as its last segments emerged. It left her stretched and exhausted. She fell back into the pond, her face just above the waterline, her breath ragged and wheezing. Smaller leeches covered more of her body, eager to dine on whatever she had left.

His knees in the water, Trevor held Little Lugosi. The air around him glowed with an unearthly orange, an effect of the sun's last rays. Somewhere, a frog croaked. Trevor needed both of his arms as Little Lugosi twisted about like an overfed cat struggling to find the best, most comfortable position. What it really wanted was skin to latch onto. When it found what it sought, it felt to Trevor like railroad spikes driving into his flesh.

"I want to see him. Give him to me."

He barely heard Madeline speak. Lying in the water with her eyes closed, she held out her arms.

"You too," she said. "Both of you, together. Come to me."

Trevor wanted to rip apart the thing he held. The prongs of the leech held him fast so he couldn't tear it away. The pain made him dizzy. On the shore, the Minister stopped rooting around so it could witness the conclusion of Trevor's midwifery. Trevor looked at Madeline, his sweet, unpredictable Madeline. She repeated what she said.

Trevor made sure she could still breathe as he brought himself close to her. He barely felt the other smaller leeches that had found purchase on his skin. As he joined Madeline, he realized why she wanted to lie there: the water felt soothing.

With the other half of his body, Little Lugosi found Madeline and latched himself to her. In that way, it joined them both, the curve of its body conforming to theirs, pulsing with their heartbeats, luxuriating on their heat, and claiming as its own property their affection for one another.

It no longer caused pain. In fact, nothing hurt. Instead, a different, more puzzling feeling began to emerge.

Euphoria.

Madeline couldn't open her eyes now, but she must've sensed how Little Lugosi joined them.

"Can you feel it?" she asked.

"I do."

As the sun continued its descent, the air around them seemed to dance. Trevor wished she could open her eyes to witness it with him.

"Rose?" she asked.

He didn't understand the question at first and wondered if she somehow mistook him for Rose.

"Is she gone?" she asked when he didn't answer.

Trevor lifted his head slightly so he could see Rose's remains on the shore. A silver cloud hovered above her, her spirit made manifest or a horde of insects, Trevor couldn't tell. Maybe it was both. Like everything else surrounding them, that silver cloud looked beautiful.

"She's gone," he said.

"I'm sorry," Madeline said. "I did what she wanted. It was supposed to feel good. I did it for us. To bring us closer. I didn't know what she really intended. We weren't supposed to be apart for so long. It was supposed to be our rebirth. The rebirth of us. You believe me, don't you?"

She lifted a limp hand and caressed Little Lugosi. Little Lugosi pulsed and flexed, probing deeper into Trevor. Through its penetration, Trevor felt that caress too. Flies made ripples in the water, and a gust of wind arose, stirring the trees and cooling everything around them.

"I believe you," Trevor said.

From out of the trees hopped a rabbit. His head still upraised and feeling somehow both heavier and lighter at the same time, Trevor watched the rabbit approach the skull of the pig once worn by Rose. After sniffing it, the rabbit hopped away, past the Minister, who continued to root around in the dirt, paying it no notice at all, as if it had decided to act like just any pig, not some feral animal god. Following the rabbit's path from the trees came a group of smaller pigs, and they joined the Minister in His rooting.

"Everything here is beautiful," Trevor said.

Still latched to their bodies, Little Lugosi reacted to the sound of his voice by flexing more. It made a sound that Trevor likened to that of a gentle kiss, almost a sigh.

When Madeline didn't answer, Trevor said, "You're beautiful. The most beautiful thing here."

Things began to grow fuzzy. He tried to focus his eyes on her so he could see her more clearly. Despite the marks and bruises and the way all these experiences had reshaped her body, she really was the most amazing thing he'd ever seen. He felt so glad she called for him to jump over the gate that day at the fair.

Trevor asked, "Do you know that?"

Still no reply from Madeline. As if distracted by something more interesting, Little Lugosi let go of Trevor with a gentleness that Trevor could hardly appreciate since he felt so little of anything now. It let go of Madeline too, and with an awkward roll of its body, it fell into the water. It took some struggle because he felt so sleepy, but Trevor managed to shift himself so he could fill the space left by Little Lugosi. He wanted every part of his body to touch

Madeline in this moment.

"You're so cold," he said, not noticing that he'd begun shivering. "I'll warm you up," he tried to say. He got most of the words out, but he might have left off the last word or two. As he huddled against Madeline in the shallows of the pond, a new movement caught his attention.

At first, he mistook it for the dead former professor. It alarmed him a bit to think Barnswallow still lived after what happened to him, what with half of his guts steaming on the ground, but he felt so guilty for leading the man to his death he wanted to rejoice in the revelation that his body still contained life.

Yet the movement didn't come from Barnswallow. Instead, he realized Little Lugosi had crawled to the edge of the pond and managed to stand up like a person, a tall black form in the expanding darkness. It stood so tall Trevor realized it must've grown considerably during the time it spent latched onto him and Madeline, reaching the size of a large human being.

How did you do that? Trevor wanted to ask. *How*

did you manage that, you amazing thing? He really wanted to know.

Then a slit appeared in its body, and it opened up, peeling back a layer of skin like a pair of wings, like a cape it wore to conceal its true form. Underneath, a human being, one with pale skin that stood out against the blackness of its cape, and a mouth stretched wide to reveal a cavern filled with sharp teeth.

That cavern grew unnaturally wider as it smiled at Trevor's recognition.

Trevor remembered where he'd seen it.

At the end of the carnival ride, the haunted house. What hid in the shadows behind the girl covered in blood.

"You," Trevor managed to say. He hugged Madeline tighter. "I'm not afraid of you. *We're* not afraid of you. Just go." And Trevor meant it. He felt no fear. Nothing would happen to him or Madeline as long as he kept the thing in the cape within his field of vision, as long as he refused to look away. "Just go," he said.

But the thing held its place there on the shore,

watching as Trevor held Madeline. Trevor took comfort in believing that despite all those teeth, it had no real power. Just a stark vision, one that marred the beauty all around them. That's all it was. Trevor kept his eyes upon it, not blinking, until the darkness around them became too much and he couldn't see anything at all.

EIGHTEEN

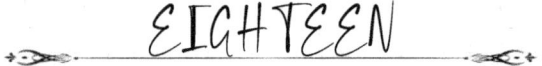

Little Lugosi swims.

Normally, its instincts would tell it to hide, to find a place where it could settle itself until it needed to feed again. Yet it feels so driven by the flesh fluid coursing through its body. Plus, this new space, all this water, so full of fresh vibrations and such different tastes that it must swim. It needs to feel all the new and different chemical reactions surrounding it, and if it could do so, it would will its body to grow and grow until it filled every crevice and felt every wave. Its underbelly scrapes a rock, and it shivers at the touch. It would return to find the rock to experience that feeling again, but then it touches a broken branch and feels a different, even more pleasurable sensation, so it just keeps swimming and swimming. Other vibrations reach it, something falling in the water perhaps, so it swims in that direction, a fat blind thing but so alive to everything around it. It has ten stomachs, all bloated yet eager for more sustenance, telling each other to swim swim swim, thirty-two brains commanding each other all at once, swim swim swim, nine pairs of testicles, all tingling, eager to burst, and adding to the chorus, swim swim swim. Such noises in that rotund body, all drowning each other out, and though it has no ears to hear, there occur two voices inside it that drive it the most, two human voices living within the blood it has ingested. Unknown to it, those voices drive it the most, those two voices it knew through the vibrations that came through a plastic container so long ago that it could never remember, even if its thirty-two brains had any notion of time. But those human voices course through Little Lugosi's blood, touch everything inside it. They, most of all, account for how alive it feels, how energetic, how stimulated it feels when it touches a moss-covered rock. It has no capacity for names or faces and certainly no capacity for love, but it knows those people, their taste still clinging to the several hundred teeth that fill its mouths, so much so that it takes a while for its energy to finally fade, causing it to slow down until finally it just floats there in the pond. Eventually, even the waters around become still. Still, something inside it persists, a dull roar inside its own body it cannot understand. It craves something it could never understand, that urge, that vibration within itself, so persistent. It comes from that borrowed blood, its food, and it wants that taste again, just one more time, the thing its own body contains.

Finally, it knows what to do.

It curls its back end, turning itself into a little ball, and with the mouth of its anterior, it seeks out the matching mouth on its posterior. Little Lugosi has never done this before and couldn't begin to understand the impulse. It just knows that it must bring those two mouths together, the teeth biting and scraping one another, latching together so that Little Lugosi forms a body with no end, no beginning. Floating, in ecstasy.

About Douglas Ford

According to Stoker Award-winning author, Tim Waggoner, Douglas Ford "wields language like a sinister surgeon with a night-black scalpel." Ford's collection of weird fiction, Ape in the Ring and Other Tales of the Macabre and Uncanny, was published by Madness Heart Press in 2020, earning praise from Owl Goingback, who called it "a must have collection for every horror library." Ford followed this collection with The Beasts of Vissaria County, a novel released by D&T Publishing in 2021. His short fiction has appeared in a wide variety of publications, from Dark Moon Digest to Diabolical Plots, and a novella, The Reattachment, appeared in 2019 courtesy of Madness Heart Press.